LOVE ON THE RUN

SUZIE TULLETT

D1612837

ALSO BY SUZIE TULLETT

The Trouble With Words

Little White Lies and Butterflies

The French Escape

Six Steps To Happiness

Holly's Christmas Countdown

A Not So Quiet Christmas

Tessa Cavendish is Getting Married

For Robert, Adam and Ben
My boys

CHAPTER 1

FOUR WEEKS UNTIL RACE DAY

"We're going to be mixing with the rich and famous." Beth giggled in excitement. "Look at this."

She and her brother sat at the dining table. They scrolled through their mobiles while their mother, Hannah, tidied up the kitchen around them.

Beth held up her phone screen. "It's a list of who's who with villas near ours."

Archie's eyes widened as he read. "Imagine walking down the road and coming face to face with loads of celebrities. That's mad."

"Beats missing Danny for."

Hannah's head jerked in her daughter's direction. Either that was one hell of a name check Beth and Archie were looking at, or Hannah had slipped over into the twilight zone. Danny Parkes was one of those singers who appealed to teenagers, mothers and grandmothers alike and along with most of the female population, Hannah's daughter idolised him.

Anyone would have thought Beth's life had ended when she realised their trip overlapped with one of his concerts. Try as she might, there was no budging on the holiday dates. The relief Beth felt when she learned the whole event had sold out and, France or no France, she wouldn't be seeing Danny anyway.

"Unless..." Beth's eyes widened, and she frantically tapped on her phone screen. "I'm sure I read somewhere that he was looking at houses down where we're going."

"Earth to children," Hannah said, bringing them back to reality. "Time to use the bathroom. Your dad and whatshername will be here soon."

Beth frowned. "Point one, you mean Monica."

"Do I?" Hannah replied. "In my defence, it's hard to keep up."

Hannah's children looked up from their phones and stared at Hannah in astonishment.

"Bitchy or what!" Archie said, trying not to snigger.

Hannah blushed, knowing Archie was right to call her out. As she emptied a stack of plates from the dishwasher, even she couldn't believe she'd just said that. In all the years following the divorce, Hannah had made sure never to say a bad word about Carl to the children, even when bad words were warranted. Plus, what her ex-husband did, with whom, and for what period was none of Hannah's business.

"I'm sorry," Hannah said. "That wasn't nice." Being fair to Monica, she hadn't just been on the scene longer than most in Carl's umpteen girlfriends, Monica obviously didn't begrudge spending time with the kids, and more importantly they seemed to like her.

"Point two," Beth continued, getting back to why she was affronted. "We're not babies."

Hannah scoffed. Didn't she know it. Unlike fifteen-year-olds, babies didn't backchat. "No, but you do have a long drive ahead of you."

Beth rolled her eyes. "Like we can't control our bladders."

Recalling the number of occasions the three of them had set out

2

in the car, only to find that twenty minutes into the drive one of them needed a pit stop, Hannah wasn't about to back down. For their own good, as opposed to hers. Having had plenty of practice, patience might have been Hannah's strong point, but it certainly wasn't their father's. "And like I can't control these," Hannah said, imitating her daughter's voice. Reaching for their passports, Hannah stared at Beth and Archie, eyebrows raised, daring them to try her.

Realising the matter wasn't up for discussion, Hannah's children groaned in protest. Their chairs scraped against the floor tiles as they got up and trudged out into the hallway, muttering to themselves as they went.

"I'm so not going to miss her," Beth said.

"Bet she'll miss us though," Archie said.

"She's probably just jealous because while we're off having fun she's stuck here."

Hannah sniggered as she got back to her domestic duties. Beth wasn't wrong. Who wouldn't want to spend a month in Provence. With its swathes of golden beaches and crystalline azure seas, not to mention its provincial towns and bustling market squares, Hannah easily envisaged herself watching the world go by over a lingering lunch and glass of Cantoiseau Blanc. Except unlike Beth and Archie's hotshot lawyer of a dad, Hannah couldn't afford it.

As for Archie's snidey comment, as much as Hannah loved her children, she was sure she'd cope with the lack of hormonal bickering, let alone not having to cook multiple meals at once because one of them had turned vegan for a week while the other most definitely hadn't. In fact, the thought of cleaning the house and it staying that way made Hannah positively giddy.

From the 17th century vase she'd picked up for £10 at a car boot sale, to the rare elm wicker chair she'd found in a junk shop, to the Chinese bamboo pot she'd got for a fiver, with Beth and Archie away, Hannah relished the prospect of delighting in all her treasures instead of focusing on schoolbags and shoes left in the middle of the floor.

Bought cheap with her divorce settlement because it was so run down, Hannah had worked hard over the years to get her home just the way she wanted. She couldn't count the number of YouTube DIY videos she'd watched and hours of graft she'd put in to save money on labour costs. Everything about her house was budget minded.

Hannah looked over at the Welsh dresser she'd previously transformed. All set to go to the tip, she'd rescued it from a neighbour. It was surprising what could be done with a bit of creativity, a sander and a pot of Farrow and Ball flat matt paint. She'd thoroughly enjoyed transforming it into the beauty it had become and finding herself with the time, Hannah wondered if she might use the next few weeks to pick up some more trash that she could turn into treasure.

She thought back to when Carl had first announced Beth and Archie's end-of-year-exams reward. It was just like him to swoop in with an over-the-top gesture. Hannah pictured the kids jumping up and down and screaming as if they'd won the lottery, leaving Hannah little choice but to stand there, hiding her annoyance behind a fake smile and clamped jaw. At the time, Hannah couldn't believe Carl hadn't discussed his plans with her first. A concern he dismissed.

It was evident Carl viewed himself as the fun parent; the one who took Beth and Archie to fancy restaurants, bought them expensive gifts and, as it turned out, arranged lavish holidays. As for getting his hands dirty, he did none of that. It seemed Carl was way too important to help with any of the mundane stuff, leaving Hannah to raise their children, clean up after them, be the disciplinarian… That was when Hannah realised the trip was a gift in more ways than one. Not only would Hannah get a break, Carl would finally learn what it was like to be a proper parent.

Hannah smirked as the sound of squabbling interrupted her thoughts.

"Those are my earphones."

"No, they're not. Give them back."

Hannah heard the two of them tussle.

"Get off!"

"Not until I get what's mine."

Hannah's smile turned into a giggle. Carl might have thought he was Father of the Year with his excessive presents and a surprise holiday but having never had the kids for more than a weekend at a time, he didn't have a clue what he'd let himself in for.

CHAPTER 2

While Beth and Archie finished upstairs, Hannah contemplated the weeks ahead. She might not have been heading for the South of France, but she still looked forward to the following few weeks. She planned on sleeping in every morning, spending days relaxing on the sofa, eating what she wanted when she wanted, and getting lost in all the books she hadn't found time to read. For once, Hannah was going to be a lady of leisure. Something she'd never been before.

Hannah cocked her head and her thoughts were interrupted when a car horn beeped followed by what sounded like a stampede as Beth and Archie charged down the stairs.

"Are you sure you have everything you need?" Taking their passports with her to give to Carl for safekeeping, Hannah headed out into the hall to see Beth and Archie sling their rucksacks over their shoulders.

"It's a bit late if we haven't," Beth replied, eager to get going.

As was Archie. "Mediterranean here we come," he said, flinging open the front door.

Grabbing their suitcases, it appeared the two of them couldn't get out of the house quickly enough.

"Excuse me," Hannah said, raising her voice.

Beth and Archie stopped.

Refusing to let them go without a proper goodbye, Hannah tapped her cheek in readiness.

Beth crumpled. "Mum, you're so needy."

"That's because she hasn't got a life," Archie said.

Hannah laughed. "And why do you think that is? Between looking after you two, running a house and going out to work, there isn't much time for anything else."

"You know what they say," Beth said. "There are twenty-four hours in a day, it's up to you how you spend them."

Hannah scoffed. She'd never heard such a privileged statement. Whoever came up with that little nugget of advice had evidently never been a single mum. "Is that so? I'll remember that the next time you're nagging for a lift."

Beth and Archie gave Hannah the briefest of hugs and quickest of kisses.

"*Now* can we go?" they both asked.

Hannah nodded and the two of them clamoured out the door, desperate to start their French adventure.

"Make sure you text me," Hannah called out.

"We will," Beth replied.

"Every few days. So I know you're alive and well."

"Bye, Mum!" Such was Archie's excitement, he almost bumped into his dad who made his way up the garden path.

"Careful!" Jumping out of the way, Carl shook his head. "Anyone would think they'd never been anywhere before."

Hannah observed her ex walk towards her. Wearing chino shorts and a tight-fitting T-shirt that showed off his broad chest and muscular arms, Carl's self-confidence shone through. His overgrown hair was pushed back off his face and a huge smile revealed perfect teeth. There was no denying Carl's good looks. Tall, blond, and with near flawless features, Hannah could see him fitting in with the South of France's elite. As would her children, she acknowledged, who took after their dad in both poise and looks.

Watching them throw their suitcases into the swanky Range Rover's boot before climbing into the back seat, Hannah missed Beth and Archie already. She didn't know whether to feel envious of, or sorry for, Monica as the two of them enthusiastically greeted her. On the plus side, Monica didn't appear fazed by Beth and Archie's exuberance. She seemed to match it, which Hannah considered a good sign.

"Are you ever going to get rid of that?" Carl indicated the huge lion statue sat to the right of Hannah's front door. "It's so bloody ugly."

"In China, stone lions act as guardians. They're said to defend homes from accidents and theft." Hannah could see Carl didn't care one way or the other, but she carried on anyway. "Buddhists think they bring peace and prosperity, while in Italy they symbolise power and prestige."

Carl shook his head. "So in other words, no."

"Of course it's a no. I think he's gorgeous. Besides, he's famous around these parts. A real talking point. People would miss him if I got rid of him." She patted the statue's head. "Wouldn't they, Leo?" She returned her attention to Carl ready to get down to business. "Beth and Archie won't get far without these." Hannah handed over their passports. "I'm giving them to you because I know they'll only lose them."

"Understood." Carl shoved the documents into his shorts pockets.

"Also, you'll need to make sure Archie wears sun lotion. He hates the stuff, says it makes his skin too greasy. He'll do anything to get out of putting it on." Anxiety began to threaten Hannah. To say she'd been looking forward to some well-earned me time, she hadn't realised how hard handing Beth and Archie over for more than a couple of days would be. "And don't let them out of your sight."

"Hannah, they're fifteen."

"Which is way too young to be wandering around a foreign country on their own. Do you want one of them to get kidnapped? Oh, and make sure they eat properly. Left up to them, it'll be pommes frites and ketchup morning, noon and night."

Carl scoffed. "Anything else?"

Hannah took a deep breath, insisting that while Carl might have a more chilled parenting style than her, he'd never put Beth and Archie at risk. "If I think of something, I'll message."

"So, what do you plan on getting up to while we're away?" Carl asked.

"You mean apart from putting my feet up, stuffing my face, and enjoying the peace and quiet?"

"For a whole month?" Carl looked at Hannah, incredulous. "Surely, you can come up with something better than that? Won't you get bored?"

Hannah laughed. The fact that he expected more doing and less sitting on her part evidenced just how little he knew about living with teenagers. "I've booked time off work especially for it."

"Come on, Dad!" Beth called out.

Carl put a hand up, acknowledging his daughter's request. "Coming, sweetheart."

Sweetheart? Hannah bit down on her lips, hoping to goodness that Monica was made of sterner stuff. If not, the only adults in the group were going to be eaten alive.

"Can I ask you something?" Hannah asked, before Carl could leave.

He shrugged. "I suppose."

"Why now? Why not take the kids away last year? Or the year before and the year before that? It's not like I've never suggested it."

Carl glanced over at the car before looking down at his feet as if not sure how to answer.

Watching him, Hannah's eyes widened in amusement. "Oh, I get it."

Carl snapped his head back up, defensive. "What do you get?"

Hannah indicated Monica. "That this thing between the two of you is serious." Hannah realised she should have known their trip to France wasn't as simple as her ex had portrayed. It had never been solely about treating Beth and Archie. It was an opportunity for them to get to know his girlfriend better; a situation Hannah never thought she'd see.

Carl blushed. "And if it is?"

Hannah let out a laugh. Carl might frustrate her on occasion, but Hannah's feelings for the man, love and loathe, had long since dissipated. She glanced over at the car again to see Beth and Archie grappling with each other in the back seat. "As long as the kids are happy, that's all I care about."

"To be fair, this was Monica's idea. She thinks I should spend some proper time with Beth and Archie, that we both should."

"Really?" Hannah was surprised and impressed. More interested in what Carl's money could buy them, none of Carl's prior girlfriends had taken his parental responsibilities that seriously.

He opened his mouth to say something else but before he got the chance he was interrupted.

"Dad!" Shoving his whole upper torso out of the car window, Archie signalled for Carl to get a move on.

"I'd better go," Carl said, turning to leave. "I'll ring you when we get there, yeah."

"Have fun." Hannah smiled as she watched him head back to his car and climb in. Having thought the day would never come, she had to wonder if love was in the air for her ex-husband.

Carl pulled the vehicle away from the kerb and waving the four of them off, Hannah stood there until they disappeared.

With them out of view, she took a deep breath, not sure what to do next. Already, things seemed strange.

Going back inside, the house immediately felt too quiet and heading for the kitchen, Hannah glanced around. For all her bravado about making the most of being home alone, she let out a long drawn-out sigh. The month ahead suddenly felt like an eternity.

CHAPTER 3

*L*etting himself through the back door and into the kitchen, Gabe headed straight to the fridge for a bottle of water. Unscrewing its lid and putting it to his lips, he squeezed the plastic, enjoying the cold liquid as it glugged down his throat. He sweated profusely and his body already started to ache. The mountainous run he'd just put himself through had been a challenge. It had forced him to dig deep with the balls of his feet and toes, all the while powering through with his arms.

As Gabe dropped the empty bottle into the recycling bin, he wanted nothing more than a cool shower. However, the sound of his dad, Roger, whistling let Gabe know the bathroom wasn't free, he'd have to wait. Tempted to sing along to Roger's tune, the lyrics to Bobby McFerrin's 'Don't Worry Be Happy' played out in Gabe's head, an earworm he knew he wouldn't be rid of for the rest of the evening. Having never liked that song, he wished his dad had better taste in music. "Cheers, Dad," Gabe said.

Gabe had to admire his dad as the whistling continued to filter down. For a man in his late seventies, Roger had a great set of lungs. In fact, he was doing brilliantly all round and Gabe readily envisaged the man stood at the bathroom mirror, running a comb through his good head of Brylcreemed hair. Gabe chuckled at the thought of his dad stepping back to admire the result.

"You've still got it, Roger," his dad was saying, at the same time clicking his tongue and pointing both index fingers at his reflection.

Finally, the whistling stopped, and Gabe heard footsteps coming down the stairs.

"You're back," Roger said, his face lighting up as he entered the kitchen. "I didn't hear you come in."

"I'm not surprised with all the hoot tooting going on."

"What do you think?" Stood there in a navy suit, white shirt, and dark blue tie with a contrasting pink flamingo print, Roger held his arms out. Wiggling his hips as he went, he did a 360-degree turn to show himself off in all his glory.

A surge of aftershave scent flew in Gabe's direction, and he tried not to cough. "Very smart. Who's the lucky lady?"

"Brianna Dawson."

Gabe watched his dad fill with pride as if the name alone should have meant something.

"You must remember her," Roger said, clearly disappointed Gabe didn't. "Blonde, curvaceous, beautiful eyes…" He paused as if waiting for something to click. "A member of the golf club."

With nothing coming through, Gabe shook his head. "That pretty much sums up everyone you date, Dad." He grabbed another bottle of water from the fridge. "Besides, your love life isn't exactly easy to keep up with."

Straightening his back and standing tall, Roger puffed his chest out. "You know what they say, son. Variety is the spice of life."

Gabe unscrewed the bottle lid. "For you, maybe."

It was at times like this that Gabe found Roger's confidence hard to believe.

Gabe had heard stories about couples whereby one half

couldn't carry on without the other. A partner would pass away, and within months the person left behind would follow suit. Brought on by stressful situations and extreme emotions, it even had a name. Broken Heart Syndrome. When his mum had died, for a while, Gabe had thought his dad might succumb to his loss.

Gabe recalled how for months afterwards, if Roger wasn't laying on his bed next to where his wife had slept, he was sat in her chair going through old photograph albums. Getting Roger to eat had been a struggle, let alone coaxing him out of the house. It was as if Roger had completely given up on life.

It was a period Gabe still found difficult to think about and were it not for the support group Gabe had eventually dragged Roger kicking and screaming to, Gabe genuinely believed he'd have gone on to lose both parents, not just one.

"Is there any point in me enquiring about your plans for tonight?" Roger asked.

"I'm meeting up with Slim, if that's what you're asking."

Roger's shoulders slumped. "It's not and you know it's not."

Gabe felt bad for disappointing his dad, but the last thing he wanted to do was play the dating game. "I get that you mean well, but–"

Roger put a hand up to silence Gabe. He indicated they take a seat at the table.

Gabe had heard it all before and telling himself God loves a trier, did as he was told. Placing his arms on the table, he clasped his hands. It was conversation they'd had numerous times and it always ended with the same result.

"Look, I know you think I don't understand," Roger began. "That it's easy for me to have an opinion."

Happy to let his dad ramble, Gabe settled himself down for the long haul.

"And Lord knows, I've already spent what most people consider a lifetime with the most beautiful woman a man could wish to meet."

Gabe smiled at his mum's memory.

"Yes, I go out and have fun, but after your mother, I'm not looking for a partner. For me, life's about making the most of my twilight years. Enjoying good food, great conversation, and… well, you know."

Gabe shuddered. He didn't want to even think about his dad's sex life.

"I suppose what I'm trying to say, Gabe, is it's been two years now. Don't you think it's time to move on? To give yourself a chance to find what me and your mum had?"

Gabe appreciated the concern, however misplaced. "I have moved on, Dad. Honestly."

Roger sighed. But it wasn't a sign of defeat. "Tell you what, why don't I postpone Brianna so we can have a boys' night out? I can give you some tips. Even better, you can see them in action."

Gabe's eyes widened in horror.

"And I'm more than happy to be your wingman. In fact, thinking about it, we'd make a great team."

Trying not to picture the scene, Gabe let out a laugh. "Thanks for the offer, Dad. But I'm good."

"What *can* I do to help then?" Roger gestured to Gabe's running shoes and sportswear. "In case you've forgotten, there *are* better forms of exercise, you know."

Again, Gabe shuddered. "Have you ever considered I might be content with the way things are?"

"Nope." It seemed Roger wasn't for budging.

Gabe got up from his seat. "Then maybe it's time you did."

"I haven't considered it because despite what you say, you're not happy, son." Roger folded his arms and leant back in his seat. "I know you better than you think."

"Trust me, Dad." Picking up his bottle of water, Gabe patted his dad's shoulder. "I'm absolutely fine."

Roger sneered but it was to no avail.

Ready to end the conversation once and for all, Gabe exited the room and headed upstairs for his much-needed shower.

CHAPTER 4

*H*annah locked the front door behind her and hastened down the garden path to her car. Climbing in, she threw her bag down on the passenger seat. Flustered, she took a deep breath to calm herself before starting up the engine. Sticking the vehicle into gear, she slammed on the accelerator and headed into town.

She couldn't believe she was running late. Fed up with her own company, it turned out having a spotless house in which to admire her treasures wasn't all it was cracked up to be and as the one to suggest that evening's soiree, the least Hannah thought she could do was get there on time.

She crossed her fingers as she approached a set of traffic lights, willing them to stay green. She groaned in frustration as they turned red, leaving her no choice but to bring her car to a standstill. Finally, they went from red to amber, but a teenage boy stepped out preventing Hannah from moving. "You've got to be kidding me," she said, as the boy dawdled across the road.

Finally able to get going again, Hannah drummed her fingers on the steering wheel as she drove. She normally had an excuse for running late; Beth not coming out of piano practice on time;

Archie's football match going to penalties; both of them too busy having fun with their friends to realise their personal taxi was at the door. With no such justification that evening, it seemed time management was an issue even when it needn't be.

At last, she arrived at her destination and spotting a streetside parking space, she swung in her car, while at the same time hitting the brakes. Screeching to a halt, she pulled her keys free of the ignition and retrieved her bag. Flinging her door open, it seemed to hit something and immediately bounce back. "What the...?" Hannah only just stopped it from crashing into her leg. She pushed on the car door for a second time, and climbing out spotted a man, who stood there grimacing and rubbing his thigh.

"Oh no, I'm so sorry," Hannah said. His injuries were obviously her fault. "Are you okay?" she asked, mortified.

Despite Hannah's apology, the man continued to frown.

"Your wing mirrors are there for a reason," he said.

Hannah regarded him for a moment. Tall, dark and handsome, the man's looks were better than his manners. "And so are the eyes in your head," she replied, noting his were of the deepest brown. She pursed her lips, before turning her attention to her car. "I hope you haven't damaged my door."

"Excuse me?"

She made a point of checking it over. "Well, we have just established you weren't looking where you were going."

"We've just what?" The man stared at Hannah as if not quite believing what he was hearing. "You do know pedestrians have the right of way, right?"

"I know some pedestrians need to be more careful."

Seeing the man's frustration, Hannah guessed he wasn't used to being challenged. Although she appreciated why. She'd read numerous research articles on how good-looking people were often treated more favourably. Not that Hannah had any inclination to be nice. After all, he hadn't even tried to accept her apology. "Have you ever heard of the beauty premium?" she naughtily asked, instead.

Opening and closing his mouth, the man looked at her confused. He seemed to have trouble articulating, something Hannah didn't have time for.

Watching him, he reminded Hannah of Beth and Archie, who wore the same bewildered expression whenever she'd cause to play word games with them. "Now if you don't mind," Hannah said, when the man's words continued to evade him. "I'm already running late."

Locking the car door, she dropped her keys into her bag and leaving the man stood there, Hannah stuck her nose in the air and went on her way.

CHAPTER 5

"*H*annah! Over here!"

Hearing her name, Hannah glanced through the crowds until she spotted Mel who waved her way. Such was Hannah's timekeeping, she'd half expected to find herself deserted for the evening and with no desire to go back to an empty house, relief swept over her.

Mel pointed to three glasses of wine sat on the table in front of her, mouthing to let Hannah know she didn't need to queue at the bar.

Pleased to see it, Hannah put her thumb up in gratitude. She squeezed through various groups of partygoers, forced to contend with the pungent mix of aftershave and perfume assaulting her nostrils as she went. She'd almost forgotten what it was like to be in a busy night-time pub and trying not to step on people's toes, she knew if she'd had to get her own drink, she wouldn't have had any left by the time she reached Mel; she'd have spilt it all. "Sorry I'm late." She gave her friend a hug before taking a seat. "Time sort of ran away with me."

"Doing what?" Mel laughed. "I thought Beth and Archie were on holiday."

"I do have a life outside of being a mum."

Mel raised an eyebrow.

Hannah crumpled. Having wanted to be just like one of those parents who jumped for joy on their children's first day back at school, she'd had to keep busy to stop herself from missing hers the second they'd left for France. "All right, I admit it. I'm lost without them."

Mel gave Hannah a sympathetic, yet amused, smile.

"They've only been gone a couple of days and I've already run out of things to do." Hannah showed Mel her hands. "Look. They're still raw from all the scrubbing I did cleaning the house from top to bottom. I've been to the supermarket and now have a packed fridge-freezer and fit-to-burst cupboards. I'm telling you, when you're not used to it, shopping for one is a lot harder than you think." Hannah sighed. She'd tossed way too many comfort buys into the trolley and had ended up with enough supplies to last a family of ten, never mind three, for the following six months.

Mel went from half empathising to looking at Hannah like she'd gone mad. "You do know you're mental, right?"

"Oh, it gets worse. I've washed all the bedding, got through the laundry from the basket. And with no more chores left, spent the last few hours distracting myself with my first TV binge." Hannah picked up her drink. "I got lost in that Netflix detective show you and Liv are always talking about. That's why I'm late." She took a sip. "Now I know why, when the kids are watching something, instead of turning off the TV when I ask, I'm met with pleas of *just one more episode*."

"Have you heard from them?" Mel asked.

"Carl rang to let me know they landed okay and I've had a couple of messages." Hannah frowned. Her children were obviously having way too much fun to think about her. "But nothing else."

Hannah decided to change the subject and pointed to the

untouched wine glass. "Where's Liv? It's not like her to be behind." Hannah's punctuality might not have a great track record, but Liv's was impeccable.

"I'm surprised you didn't see her on your way in. She's outside somewhere. Talking to her new boyfriend."

"Liv has a new boyfriend? Since when?"

Mel nodded. "Oh, yes."

Something in Mel's eyes told Hannah there was more to come on the subject.

"He texted, so she went to give him a call."

"Really?" Hannah's surprise intensified. The Liv she knew liked to keep her men dangling. "Things must be serious. Who is he? How did they meet?"

"I thought my ears were burning," Liv said, a glint in her eye as she appeared at the table. She gave Hannah a hug and sat down. "That's what happens when you skive off work. You miss out on all the juicy gossip."

"Excuse me, I'm on holiday leave."

"Hannah, holidays involve sun, sea, and sand." Liv picked up her glass and drank a mouthful of wine. "Not slobbing around at home in your pyjamas all day."

Hannah pictured herself earlier that afternoon, feet up on the sofa, stuffing biscuit after consoling biscuit into her mouth. "Have you been spying on me?"

"For what it's worth, I think you should cancel your break and come back to work," Mel said.

Admittedly, the idea had crossed Hannah's mind. But after all the gloating she'd done about making the most of being a lady of leisure for a change, despite the rant she'd just had she wasn't about to turn thoughts into action.

"You know they've put Francesca on our team," Mel continued. "And that we're stuck with her until you do?"

"Don't remind me," Liv said. "If that woman tells me I'm not reaching my target one more time, I swear I'll swing for her."

Working at a banking call centre wasn't exactly the best job in the world, especially in a department like Hannah's. Life had a habit of throwing curveballs; curveballs that changed people's circumstances and dealing with customers who could no longer meet their financial obligations could be emotionally draining. Like Hannah, Mel and Liv cared more about what they could do to help customers than they did the number of calls they took in an hour. Hannah grimaced. Then there was Francesca. Image conscious and ambitious, she was determined to climb the ranks and be it a customer or colleague, she didn't care who she stamped on to get there.

"Enough about her," Hannah said. "We're here to enjoy ourselves." She turned her attention to Liv. "I'm more interested in this new man of yours."

Liv's face lit up as she prepared to tell all, while Mel sucked in her lips as if trying not to laugh.

Hannah looked from one woman to the other, curious.

"His name's Quentin," Liv said, ready to rhyme off her new beau's attributes. "He's the same age as me and lives local to here. He works for a non-profit. And he's so handsome, you wouldn't believe."

Considering Liv's prior partners, Hannah didn't doubt that for one second.

Mel let out a chuckle. "And... what else is he?"

Hannah took in Mel's hilarity and wondering what lay behind it, her interest piqued.

Liv smirked. "He's a vegan."

"No!" Hannah put a hand against her chest. "But you're a–"

"Farmer's daughter," Liv said, before Hannah could finish.

"Add to that the fact that she doesn't only eat steak, she orders it blue." Mel's glee continued. "It's a match made in heaven, wouldn't you say?"

"So where did you meet him?" From what Hannah had just heard she doubted Liv and Quentin ran in the same circles.

"At the supermarket," Liv said.

Mel further giggled. "Ah, but when at the supermarket?"

"You mean there's more?"

"Oh, yes," Mel said.

Liv swallowed, as if trying to keep a straight face. "I met him during singles hour."

Hannah tried and failed to keep her composure. "I didn't know they still did those things."

"Neither did I," Liv said. "I only went in for some milk."

"Cow's milk," Mel added.

"Did *he* know it was singles hour?" Hannah asked, her voice breaking.

Liv shrugged. "I didn't ask."

Hannah clamped down on her jaw.

"It's all right," Liv said. "You're allowed to see the funny side."

"I'm sorry," Hannah said. "At least you're in a relationship. My love life's been non-existent for years."

"I'm not sorry." Mel's amusement continued. "I think it's hilarious."

"Tell me about the non-profit Quentin works for," Hannah said, attempting a more serious approach to the conversation.

"It's something to do with recycling. Clothes and whatnot. Although his good works don't end there." Liv shone with pride. "He's off to Africa next month to help build schools."

"Very commendable," Hannah replied.

"It's one of the things we have in common."

"What is?" Hannah put her glass to her lips.

"Our charity work, of course."

Hannah suddenly choked on her drink, spraying it everywhere, while Mel burst into a guffaw.

"What?" Liv asked, evidently surprised by the response. "I do my bit."

"Dressing up for Children in Need and shaking a collection bucket isn't quite the same as volunteering abroad," Mel said.

"At least I do *something*. What do you two do?"

"I have a direct debit set up for the Dogs Trust," Hannah said, as she wiped herself down.

"And I buy the *Big Issue* every month," Mel said.

Hearing their efforts said out loud, they looked at each other. None of them could deny their efforts were pathetic.

Liv face lit up. "You know what this means, don't you?"

"That we're *all* rubbish at this giving business," Hannah said.

"That you're dating a saint," Mel said.

"It means we need to up our game." Liv rose from her seat and picked up their empty glasses with a flourish. "How else am I going to impress Quentin?" She smiled. "Same again, is it?"

Hannah watched Liv head straight to the bar. "Since when did Liv need to impress anyone? It's like she's a different person."

Mel sighed. "Love can do funny things to a woman."

"She's going to come up with some madcap idea, isn't she?"

"You can put money on it."

Hannah sighed at the prospect. "And you think *I'm* mad."

CHAPTER 6

*G*abe had hoped to walk off the pain but even as he got to the pub, he could still feel the impact of the car door slamming against his leg. As for the woman responsible, he couldn't believe her cheek. The more she'd refused to take responsibility, the more frustrating their exchange had felt. Thinking about it, he supposed it was hilarious too. The way the woman had batted off his complaints without even pausing for breath was inspirational. Talk about quick minded.

Gabe ordered a pint and looking around trying to locate his mate, Slim, he instead spotted a group of women who were clearly weighing him up. He noticed a couple of them nudged each other as if preparing to approach and he immediately turned his back on them hoping they'd stay put. Gabe had already had one awkward exchange with a member of the opposite sex that evening, he didn't want another.

The barmaid placed Gabe's drink in front of him and digging into his pocket for the money to pay for it, Gabe handed it over. "Thank you," he said. "Keep the change."

"Great," a voice said. "You're still here."

Gabe spun round again, pleased to find Slim had finally

arrived. He gave him a bear hug that included a couple of back slaps. "What took you?" Gabe asked.

"The girlfriend's keeping me busy."

Gabe grimaced. He didn't want to know.

"Not in that way," Slim said, laughing. "I'm talking in general." Slim nodded to the barmaid. "Usual, please." He turned his attention back to Gabe. "It's about time you got yourself a woman, mate."

Gabe let out a laugh. Having been there and done that, if there was one thing Gabe had learned, it was when it came to relationships, he was better off on his own.

"You've forgotten what you're missing."

"That's the problem; I haven't."

As Slim continued to grin, Gabe didn't think he'd seen his friend so happy. Yes, Slim had had other women in his life over the years, but Gabe could tell his latest connection was different. Usually he was work, work, work, stressed out at trying to fix the world one step at a time. The Slim stood next to him was more relaxed. He was enjoying life again. Having fun. If he didn't know any better, Gabe would have said Slim was in love.

Slim indicated a free table and happy to head over, Gabe winced thanks to his leg. He could already see the huge bruise he was going to wake up with.

"What's up with you?" Slim asked.

"A woman flung her car door into me."

"Ouch!" Slim grimaced as they took their seats. "You should be a bit quicker on your feet."

Taking a drink of his pint, Gabe smiled to himself. The woman who'd done it had a feistiness he found impressive. She was obviously as mad as a box of frogs though, some of what she said made no sense. "Do you know anything about a beauty premium?" he asked his friend.

Slim thought for a moment then shook his head. "Never. Why?"

"The woman who hit me asked if I'd heard of it." Gabe couldn't help but smirk as he pictured her telling him off for not watching where he was going and then storming off. Surprised she hadn't strained a neck muscle or bumped into something trying, he wondered how anyone could hold their head that high *and* see where they were going. It was a skill he certainly didn't possess.

"Looks like she made an impact in more ways than one," Slim said, knowingly.

Gabe fast shook away his train of thought. "Wishful thinking on your part, mate." As he sat enjoying his pint, the pub door swung open, and Gabe automatically looked over. Wondering if his assailant was amongst them, he scanned the faces of the group that entered. Seeing she wasn't, he frowned.

Slim shook his head. "Man, you've got it bad."

"What do you mean?" Gabe asked. "Got *what* bad?"

Slim let out a laugh, as if having none of it. "Admit it, you were looking for her, weren't you?"

Gabe felt himself blush. "Damn right I was." He picked up his drink again. "If she does come in, I want to know I can avoid her."

CHAPTER 7

"So, tell me, how're things with you?" Hannah asked, as she and Mel waited for Liv to come back from the bar. Having established her own failure at being a lady of leisure and caught up with Liv's unexpected news, Hannah thought it only right Mel spilled the tea on what she'd been up to of late. Mel was also in a new relationship and thanks to her almost-daily update at work, Hannah didn't just miss their conversations, she felt invested.

"Okay," Mel replied, non-committal. "You know."

Taking in her friend's lack of spirit, Hannah narrowed her eyes. Mel wasn't usually a woman of few words and Hannah wondered if she should be worried. "And Russel?" Hannah asked, deciding to probe further. "Is he okay too?"

Usually, the mere mention of Russel's name would be enough to make Mel's face light up. However, on that occasion, her expression remained flat. "He's fine."

Hannah grew concerned. "You know you can talk to me, right?"

"I do."

Hannah gave Mel a nudge. "Go on then."

Mel relented. "If you must know, he still hasn't asked for a video call, never mind an actual date. Hint after hint, and still, he says nothing." She sighed, mournful. "I'm starting to worry he isn't quite who he says he is."

Hannah's heart went out to Mel. Her friend had met Russel in a chat room and what had started out as two people sharing a love of old films, quickly turned into a deeper, more personal relationship. Hannah rubbed Mel's arm, appreciating her concern. With two teenage children, Hannah had done her internet safety research and there were so many weirdos out there creating fictional personas, it was impossible to know who was genuine and who was catfishing. Not that then was the time to remind Mel of that, Hannah realised. Mel looked anxious enough. "Then why don't *you* suggest it?" Hannah said instead. "Rather than skirt around the issue, ask him out direct."

Mel looked at Hannah, horrified. "Oh, I couldn't."

"Why not?"

"What if he says no?"

Hannah had never understood Mel's lack of confidence when it came to men. Fifteen years after giving birth, Hannah still hadn't got rid of her mummy tummy, and she'd have given anything to have Mel's perfect Marilyn Monroe figure. Of course, as well as being stunning, Mel was smart, funny, and vivacious. Russel, if indeed that was his name, might not have seen Mel in person, but from her words alone he had to know how lucky he was. "And what if he says yes?"

Mel shook her head. "I can't risk it. If I push things, I might not hear from him again. You probably think I'm soft, but I really do like Russel. I'm not sure I could cope without our nightly chats."

"But at least if you ask, you'll–"

"Tell you what," Mel said, jumping in. "How about I think about it?"

Hannah relented, knowing when to shut up. The last thing

she wanted was to bully Mel into something she didn't want to do. "Fair enough."

Mel indicated the bar area, from which Liv approached. "Please don't say anything," Mel whispered. "I might not be feeling the love right now, but that doesn't mean I want to spoil her excitement."

Watching Mel straighten herself up and put on a happy face, Hannah followed suit. That was another thing about Mel, Hannah acknowledged. She always put everyone else ahead of herself.

Liv grinned as she placed a tray of drinks down on the table. "I've only gone and found the answer!"

"The answer to what?" Mel asked.

Liv handed out the glasses. "Our charity woes."

"I didn't realise we had any," Hannah said.

"Not anymore we don't." Liv produced three colourful leaflets she'd had tucked under her arm. "I found these at the bar next to one of those collection tins." Handing two out, she kept the last for herself. "They have a stack of them."

As Liv took a seat, Hannah began to read. "Please tell me this is a joke."

Liv looked at her, incredulous. "It most certainly is not."

"Ooh, a sponsored run." Mel's eyes lit up. "What a fun idea."

Hannah stared at Mel, wondering what was wrong with the woman. Not only had the prospect of physical exercise transformed her back into her usual happy self, the words *fun* and *run* did not belong in the same sentence.

"Don't look so worried, Hannah," Liv said. "It's only 5k and we're all fit and healthy."

It seemed Hannah's friends had gone mad. "Speak for yourself."

"Liv, it's 5k over hill and dale. Look, it's being held at Wethersham Hall." Hannah had visited Wethersham Hall too many times to count. When they were growing up, it had been one of Beth and Archie's favourite picnic spots. Its grounds were vast and looking at the leaflets map, the running route cut mainly through Wethersham's woodland. Not the easiest of terrains to walk on, never mind anything faster.

Mel's excitement grew. "Did I ever tell you I hold the Saint Hilda's long-distance running record?"

"No," Liv said. "That's fantastic."

"I was sixteen when I set it and I'm still unbeaten today. The thing you have to remember, ladies, is it's all in the breathing." She looked from Liv to Hannah. "Do that, and I reckon we can easily crack this."

Hannah couldn't believe Mel had no confidence when it came to men but radiated in the stuff over running. Listening to her, Hannah didn't know whether to feel sick or impressed.

She looked down at her comfortable midriff, before scanning the pictures that accompanied the leaflet's write-up. Athletic types, wearing numbered bibs and exuding happiness, stared back at her. "There's a reason you've never seen me run, you know." She felt hot, sweaty and out of breath just thinking about it.

"It's not for another four weeks yet, Hannah," Liv said. "Look." She pointed out the race date.

"Like that's gonna help."

Liv ignored Hannah's protests. "Which gives us plenty of time to train. And it's not like you have anything else on, is it? Not with Beth and Archie in France."

"You don't even have housework and shopping to distract you," Mel said, reminding Hannah of her earlier confession.

Hannah pictured the three of them outside Wethersham Hall preparing to run the race. Tall and lithe, Liv looked the epitome of fitness in her Lycra running suit and top-of-the-range trainers. Mel, eyes closed, undertook yogic breathing exercises, before jumping up and down and stretching as she got herself into the zone. Hannah hadn't even got her foot on the starting block when the race official fired her pistol. Before Hannah knew it, Liv and Mel were disappearing into the distance, while trailing well behind, she huffed and puffed, hardly able to lift her feet.

"So what do we think?" Liv asked. "Are we all up for this?"

Hannah took in Liv and Mel's eagerness. "I thought you two were my friends."

CHAPTER 8

*H*aving made it clear she wouldn't be taking part in the sponsored race, Hannah had avoided speaking to Mel and Liv. They'd texted, trying to bring her around to their way of thinking, but Hannah was having none of it. She was all for raising money, it was the running bit Hannah objected to. She shook her head at the thought. Anyone would think Mel and Liv didn't know her.

Picking up her mobile from the kitchen counter, Hannah shook her head at their persistence, and dismissing the idea altogether, made her way into the lounge. Positioning herself on the sofa, she balanced her phone against the decorative bowl that sat on the coffee table, clicking to start a video call, before making herself comfortable. Having been time checking since getting out of bed in anticipation of finally speaking to Beth and Archie, Hannah couldn't wait to hear about their trip so far and she sat in anticipation of seeing their cheerful faces as they regaled her with stories about what they'd been up to.

The ringtone continued, and Hannah glanced over at the mantel clock. At exactly 10am UK time, which meant 11am in the South of France, she couldn't understand why no one was answering. Having texted Carl first thing to arrange it, he'd assured her Beth and Archie would be ready and waiting. She ended the call and switched from Beth's number to Archie's. With no response there either, Hannah scowled in frustration and telling herself it had to be third time lucky, she decided to try ringing Carl's phone.

She was about to concede when his face suddenly appeared on the screen. "Hannah," he said, as if surprised to see her. "Is everything all right?"

She frowned. It wasn't like Carl to forget an appointment. In her experience, he was efficiency personified. "I was about to ask you the same thing."

He screwed up his face, realisation evidently dawning. "Of course. Your catch-up with Beth and Archie. Sorry, I should have remembered."

"Yes, you should. Are they there?"

"They're splashing about in the pool. Hang on a sec, I'll get them."

Carl propped up his mobile and from what little Hannah could see, the villa they'd rented was stunning. Taking in its whitewashed walls and dark wooden beams, she envisaged a natural stone floor to go with them. Light flooded into the room, Hannah guessed from huge patio doors that led out to what was, no doubt, an immaculate seating area with a swimming pool beyond.

Almost able to smell the lavender as its scent drifted on the warm morning breeze, she'd have put money on the house having pale blue shutters, the perfect backdrop for a sun-bleached natural wood dining table that seated at least six. "How the other half live," she said to the sound of her children approaching.

A part of Hannah had hoped that Beth and Archie were missing her as much as she missed them. However, going off their conversation that wasn't the case.

"I can't believe it's that time already," Beth said. "Fingers crossed she won't keep us long. We still need to shower before lunch."

"Never mind a shower," Archie replied. "I'm starving."

"Ew. You're disgusting," Beth said.

Hannah thought it just like her son to be thinking of his stomach. He was at that age when opening the fridge door was a reflex action and no amount of food could satisfy him. "Don't worry," Hannah said, as they came into view and sat down. "I'm only making sure you're both alive and well."

"Sorry, Mum, you weren't meant to hear that," Beth said. "It's just that we've got a table booked." Her eyes widened. "We're off to La Mayssa." Talking with her hands as much as she was her mouth, La Mayssa was obviously the place to be. "It's in Villefranche-sur-Mer and has views that look out over the Mediterranean Sea."

Archie appeared equally impressed. "Honestly, Mum, after the restaurants we've been to, I'm never eating at Pizza Hut again."

Looking at them, Hannah was glad to see Carl had taken her advice on the sun cream. Instead of being lobster red, Beth and Archie's skin had warm golden undertones. Her long hair and his short curls had developed sun-kissed highlights. Bright-eyed and wearing big smiles, they looked happy and healthy. The South of France was evidently good for them.

"I'm never coming home," Beth said. "I love it here. Yesterday, we went to Cannes. Forget the film festival, it's got this beachside boardwalk called La Croisette. It's lined with a tonne of flagship stores." She came over all dreamy. "Gucci, Chanel, Dior, Louis Vuitton... they're all there. I've never seen anything like it." She snapped back into the room. "And neither has Monica. I've already told her and dad what I want for Christmas."

Envisaging Beth and Monica excitedly going from one exclusive shop to another, Hannah felt a stab of jealousy. Beth flat out refused to be seen clothes shopping with Hannah. In Beth's view, Hannah wasn't cool enough. "And how did your dad respond to that? It's only August."

"He said he and Monica will take it under consideration."

Well, well, well, Hannah thought. Things between Carl and Monica *were* serious. Not only was December months away, the two of them planned on joint gift giving.

Hannah turned her attention to Archie. "What about you?" Hannah knew from experience traipsing from shop to shop to shop, designer or otherwise, wasn't her son's thing. "What did you get up to while your sister was planning ahead?"

"Dad and I checked out the marina. You wouldn't believe how many super yachts there are around here, Mum. And owned by some pretty important people. Most of them had security men guarding the gang planks. I'm telling you, no one gets on board without their say so."

"Dad suggested *we* might be able to hire a boat at some point," Beth said.

"Not like the ones we saw in Cannes though, obviously."

"Obviously," Hannah replied. Seeing their laughter, it was good to know they were properly enjoying themselves.

"I'm not sure you'd like it here though, Mum," Beth said, turning serious.

Hannah cocked her head, wondering what made her daughter think that.

"It's very high-end. You know, glamorous."

"I can do glamorous." Hannah looked down at her jeans and T-shirt. "When it's called for."

Beth raised her eyebrows. "Mum, you wear hardly any make-up, and you never go to the hairdressers. You wouldn't know a Prada handbag if someone hit you over the head with it."

Hannah couldn't deny Beth was right.

"And everyone in France is so friendly," Archie said.

"What, and I'm not?" Hannah asked, becoming increasingly affronted.

"People here kiss complete strangers," Archie added, failing to register Hannah's question.

"On the cheeks, of course, not the lips. And only in informal settings," Beth said. She flicked her hair off her face. "In France, it's traditional."

Hannah felt her hackles rise. It was one thing her children seeing her as scruffy, but for them to think she was culturally unaware as well. "*La bise*," she said, wanting to prove them wrong.

"Excuse me?" Beth replied.

"*La bise*. That's what the kissing thing's called." Hannah could see the two of them didn't believe her.

Archie pulled his phone from his pocket and typed something in. "She's right, you know."

Hannah let out a laugh. Of course she was. She wouldn't have said it otherwise.

He held the screen towards Beth. "Look."

Beth narrowed her eyes as she read, clearly questioning how Hannah could possibly know that. "And I thought Dad was the clever one."

Hannah scoffed. "I'm not a complete numpty."

"No, but it's not like you ever go anywhere to learn these things," Beth said.

"It's not like you do anything," Archie said.

Wondering how their conversation had gone from designer shops and super yachts to her being an uneducated amoeba, Hannah straightened herself up in her seat. "Then you'll be pleased to know I'm signing up for a sponsored charity run," she said, without thinking. "How's that for getting up off my backside?"

As soon as the words were out, Hannah regretted them. Up until then, she had no intention of taking part; something she'd made very clear to Mel and Liv. Silently questioning why she suddenly felt the need to impress her own children, Hannah cursed herself for not keeping her mouth shut.

"You're doing what?" Beth asked.

"Now that I've got to see," Archie said.

Hearing them mock her, Hannah's expression froze. She wondered when her children had become so disrespectful. "What are you laughing at?"

"Mum, you can't run for a bus, never mind for money," Beth said.

Her daughter might be right, but Hannah wasn't going to tell her that.

"You don't even own a pair of trainers," Archie said.

All things considered, Hannah knew that was the least of her problems.

"What's so funny?" Carl asked, suddenly appearing at their side.

"Mum's signed up for a sponsored run," Beth said.

Carl looked at Hannah like she'd gone mad. "Really? Why? What happened to sitting on your rear for a whole month?"

"Why not?" Hannah asked, trying to sound chirpy as she pictured herself gasping for air and leopard crawling towards a finishing line.

"No reason," he replied, although Carl had never been any good at hiding his true feelings. He clearly found the prospect as hilarious as Beth and Archie did.

Hannah knew it wasn't their intention to insult her, but that didn't make their responses any less hurtful. Yes, Carl might have a fantastic salary and provide their children with fine dining and flash holidays thanks to his brilliant high-flying career, but they all knew Hannah was the one who'd kept Beth and Archie fed and watered over the years.

It was Hannah who helped them with their homework and nursed them when they were sick. She ferried them to and from sports and music events and acted like a taxi service when they spent time with their friends. All the while holding down a day job. Her heart sank. Put like that, she supposed it was no wonder they saw her as boring and predictable.

Hannah continued to stare at the three of them and taking in their shared amusement, she wasn't sure how to respond. In the last sixty seconds she'd basically been called uncultured, uninformed, and lazy. She didn't just feel like a joke, she suddenly felt like an outsider.

Not that she told them that. The last thing Hannah wanted was to ruin Beth and Archie's holiday. "I should go," she said instead. "Then you can all get ready for lunch."

As the call came to an end, Beth and Archie couldn't get away quick enough and after saying their goodbyes, Hannah continued to stare at the suddenly faceless screen. She felt a defiance well in her belly and snatching up the phone, frantically typed in a message. "I'll show you," she said of Beth, Archie, and Carl, before firing it off to Mel and Liv.

Re: the race

Hannah's text said.

I'm in!

CHAPTER 9

*G*abe sat at the kitchen table with a cup of tea. The only sound in the room was the wall clock's rhythmic tick tock. Gabe loved having his dad around. Roger moving in had been the best decision for them both. They enjoyed each other's company and had fallen into a comfortable routine. However, his dad had such an energetic approach to everything, quiet moments were few and far between. When they did come around, Gabe made the most of them.

Even getting lost in a film was a thing of the past on account of Roger's incessant talking. From the second the opening credits started, right through to *The End* the man never seemed to shut up. Roger played music and sang whenever he cooked a meal, which was often. When he did the dishes he waved a knife like it was a conductor's baton. And he often pretended to hold his wife and dance her through the house just like he'd done when she was alive. Gabe sighed, wistful. Roger might have developed an eye for the ladies, but his heart still very much belonged to the woman he'd married.

Pulling himself together, Gabe checked the time and wondered when Roger would be back; he knew his dad would insist on relaying every conversation with every person he'd talked to the second he walked in. Gabe shook his head at the prospect. No wonder he had to relish the calm whenever he got the chance.

His thoughts turned to the woman who'd slammed her car door into his thigh the other evening. As if his leg hadn't been hurting enough. His body continued to ache following the uphill challenge he'd put himself through earlier that same day and Gabe still felt embarrassed at the way he'd had to massage his leg in front of her. He cringed, realising he must have looked like one of those premier league footballers who dropped to the ground and rolled in agony at the slightest nudge from an opposing player.

Picturing the woman, Gabe couldn't help but smile and remembering Slim's observation, his friend had been right to think Gabe liked her. Short, blonde, and feisty, Gabe found her interesting and admittedly, attractive. He'd never met anyone so adept at twisting every word that came out of his mouth. Talk about quick-witted. The woman had to be an intellectual genius.

He recalled the strange question she'd asked him and intrigued as to what she was talking about, he pulled out his phone and typed *beauty premium* into its internet search bar. His eyes widened at the cheek of the woman. However, the more he read, the more his smile grew. "So you think I'm good looking too, do you?"

"Morning, son."

Having not heard the front door go, Gabe jumped at Roger's sudden appearance. He put a hand up to his chest, laughing. "Bloody hell, Dad, you nearly gave me a heart attack."

Roger glanced around the room, curious. "Who were you talking to just now?"

"Myself," Gabe replied.

Roger scoffed. "I suppose it comes to us all eventually." He handed over a white envelope. "The postman's been. This was on the doormat."

As he scanned its front, the handwriting alone told Gabe all he needed to know. Immediately recognising it, his stomach suddenly felt like lead and his smile vanished along with his good mood. Taking a deep breath, he glowered as he put the envelope down on the table.

"Aren't you going to open it?" Roger asked.

"Nope."

Roger furrowed his brow. "How come?"

Ignoring the question, Gabe got up from his seat, scraping his chair against the floor as he did so.

"Where are you going?" Roger asked, bemused.

"To get changed."

"Why?"

"I need some air."

"Gabe!"

Exiting the kitchen, Gabe heard his dad call out. Not wanting to talk to anyone, Gabe ignored him.

CHAPTER 10

*H*annah yawned as she put the kettle on and made a cup of tea. She hadn't properly slept thanks to all the tossing and turning she'd done. Brought on by Beth, Archie, and Carl's response to the idea of her taking part in a charity race, Hannah might not have challenged them at the time, but she could still hear the imaginary conversations that had played through her head during the small hours.

"What do you mean I don't do anything? Who do you think makes sure you have everything you need? Cooks your meals? Cleans up after you? As for googling *La Bise*? Do you know how insulting that is?" In Hannah's mind's eye, Beth and Archie protested, of course. They insisted they hadn't meant to offend. But when Hannah refused to accept their excuses, their smiles faded. Her children ended up apologising and seeing the error of their ways.

"As for you, Carl," Hannah went on. "You wouldn't be the hotshot lawyer you've become were it not for me." She didn't know whether it was despite Carl's profession or because of it, but even in her imagination her ex was harder to convince. Probably because in the real world, he'd never been one to face facts. Hannah gloated, enjoying a sense of one-upmanship as she sipped her tea. Ultimately, he too was no match for her imaginary self. By the time she'd finished his roasting, she didn't think she'd ever seen him so sheepish.

Of course, fantasy exchanges were all well and good, but Hannah knew their slights didn't stem from her parental duties. How could they? She was faultless on the home front. Beth, Archie, and Carl were referring to Hannah's lack of social activity and to be fair to them, aside of meeting up with Liv and Mel occasionally, they were right. She did nothing. But that was why Hannah had expected at least some encouragement when it came to the sponsored run. She looked down at her attire. And why she was dressed in jogging pants, a T-shirt, and had her hair tied into a ponytail.

She placed her cup on the kitchen counter. Hannah might not have had her children's support but that didn't mean she couldn't be her own cheerleader. Heading out into the hall, Hannah made her way upstairs. "Who's laughing now?" she asked, pausing outside Beth's bedroom door.

Hannah giggled like a naughty schoolchild as she turned the handle and entered. She knew Beth would have a fit at her snooping around in her personal space, but to be fair it was Beth's fault. If she, Archie, and Carl hadn't laughed at Hannah, Hannah would have kept shtum about the run and ergo, would've had no reason to be in there.

Glancing around, her gaze fell on a collage of photographs, each pinned to a corkboard that hung next to the dressing table. Moving in for a closer look, Hannah couldn't help but smile. They were of Beth, Archie and their friends, some of whom they'd known ever since their first day at primary. However, while they all beamed and pulled faces for the camera, a sadness washed over Hannah. She sighed, wondering where the years had gone. It didn't seem two minutes since she was their age, looking forward to the endless possibilities ahead of her. Before real life took over.

Shaking herself out of her reverie, Hannah decided to start her search by checking under the bed. She dropped to her knees and with her cheek pressed against the carpet, scanned the space. Failing to find what she was looking for, her bones creaked as she struggled back onto her feet. "Where else could they be?" Hannah turned her attention to the wardrobe.

She flung open its doors and looking inside, frowned at the cramped rail of hangers. Questioning why one girl needed so many clothes, Hannah forced them to one side and focused on the shelves below. Her face lit up. Hannah and Beth might not share the same size in dresses, but they did when it came to their feet. Hannah leant in and after rummaging through sandals, boots, wedges and pumps, she paused in delight. "Voila!" she said, at last, finding what she needed.

Pulling out a pair of trainers, Hannah sat on the mattress edge and put them on. She wiggled her feet and standing up, paced first one way and then the other. They felt a bit loose, but she told herself they'd do. No way was she spending good money on something she'd only need for a few weeks.

Hannah held her head high as she made her way back downstairs, ready to start her running journey. But as soon as she entered the kitchen her mobile rang to delay her. As she retrieved it off the counter and saw it was her mum Janice calling, she hesitated, tempted to let it ring out. The irony of the situation wasn't lost, and Hannah pictured herself that morning, sat on the sofa with her phone propped against the bowl on the coffee table. Still able to feel the frustration as she waited for Beth and Archie to pick up, Hannah clicked to answer and put the phone to her ear. "Mum, lovely to hear from you. How're things?"

"I have to say, they could be better."

Hannah put Janice on loudspeaker and setting the mobile down, grabbed a water bottle from a cupboard.

"The renovations are nowhere near where they should be by now. Although I'm not surprised considering the amount of tea these builders drink."

Hannah headed for the sink and, unscrewing the bottle lid, proceeded to fill it from the tap. "They *are* allowed a break, Mum."

"You would say that. Time wasted isn't coming out of your pocket."

"Did you ring for a reason?" Hannah asked, tightening the lid back on. "Or just to complain?"

"To ask you a favour actually."

"Go on." Hannah hoped she wasn't about to get a request to join Janice's team of painters and decorators.

"Remember Aunt Dorothy? Tall, well-built woman. In her seventies. The one with a ginormous smile."

"Of course." Having spent many a childhood summer holiday at Dorothy's down in Norfolk, Hannah couldn't believe Janice would think she'd forget. "I'm still sad about missing Uncle Denis's funeral."

Hannah recalled how she'd not been able to attend thanks to Beth and Archie being sick. They'd picked up some bug and could hardly get to the bathroom for a glass of water, never mind down to the kitchen to feed themselves. Even if Hannah had driven there and back in one day, she wouldn't have dreamt of leaving them home alone for twelve plus hours. Although, reminded of all the running up and down the stairs she did for them, Hannah couldn't help but think saying goodbye to Uncle Denis would've been easier.

"That's her." Janice lowered her voice. "Well, she's just turned up."

"What do you mean, she's just turned up?"

"In a taxi from the train station. She landed five minutes ago." Janice sighed. "Not uninvited, of course. It's just everything's been so chaotic around here these last few months, I completely

47

forgot we'd arranged it. At the time, it seemed the right thing to do considering she'd just buried her husband. I wanted to give her something to look forward to. Then we decided on the extension and as you know, the rest is history."

"She must have rung to check her stay was still on?"

"That's the thing, she did. Except your dad didn't think to tell me that."

"And you want me to step in and do what exactly?"

"I simply thought with the kids away and you rambling around that big old house of yours…"

Hannah whipped her phone off the counter, hastily took it off loudspeaker and put it to her ear. "No, Mum. Absolutely not."

"Hannah, I wouldn't ask if I had a choice." Janice's desperation came through loud and clear. "But this place is a deathtrap right now. Like I said, the builders are nowhere near finishing up. The last thing I want is Aunt Dorothy tripping over a rogue hammer and breaking a hip."

"I get that, Mum, but what am I supposed to do with her?" Hannah might be a dab hand at looking after teenagers but caring for the elderly was outside her skill set.

"Stick her in front of the telly with a fig biscuit and a mug of tea. She's brought her knitting with her. She'll be in pensioner heaven."

Hannah shook her head, hoping to goodness Dorothy couldn't hear. "Mum, as much as I'd like to help, I'm gonna have to pass."

"Why? It's not like you have anything else on. The kids aren't there."

Hannah pursed her lips, wishing people would stop saying that. "Actually, I'm going to be busy for the next few weeks."

"Doing what?" The surprise in Janice's voice was indisputable.

"I've signed up for a sponsored run."

"Excuse me?"

Hannah knew what was coming. "You heard."

"But, Hannah, you can't…"

"Run for a bus?" Hannah asked, repeating what Beth had said when she learned of Hannah's intention.

"Exactly. I mean, I know I keep on at you to get up off your bum and do something, but athleticking wasn't quite what I had in mind."

"Mum, that's not even a word. And while I might be a bit out of shape at the moment, the race isn't for a few weeks yet, which gives me plenty of time to train." Hannah eyed her water bottle. "In fact, I was just about to go for a jog when you rang."

Janice let out a laugh. "Now that I'd love to see."

"And on that note, I'm going." Hannah had heard enough insults on the matter already and she refused to listen to any more.

"But what about Aunty Dorothy?"

"Not my problem."

"We'll be over in–"

"Bye, Mum." Hannah ended the call with a sense of satisfaction.

CHAPTER 11

With her water bottle in hand and phone tucked into her pocket to monitor her progress, Hannah had a spring in her step as she set off down the street. Chest out and face forward, she smiled proudly as she jogged past the neighbouring terraces. She, and everyone else, had clearly underestimated her capabilities. "If only you could see me now," Hannah said, thinking of her growing list of naysayers.

Approaching the end of the row, Hannah winced as she felt a sharp stitch in her ribs and wondering if she'd spoken too soon, she put a hand on her hip determined to run through the pain. *It's only your body adjusting*, Hannah told herself and as she turned left onto the main road, she refused to let her confidence dwindle; a position that became increasingly difficult, as did her breathing. Struggling to get air into her lungs, Hannah questioned if a sponsored run was for her after all. She'd only been running for a few minutes and already she flagged. Cars raced by and Hannah slowed to a walk, feeling stupid for ever thinking it was.

She felt hot and bothered both physically and emotionally, and wiping the back of her hand across her sweaty forehead,

Hannah considered her options. She either humiliated herself in front of Liv, Mel, and a bunch of strangers by trying and failing to complete the event. Or suffered the embarrassment of Beth, Archie, and Carl telling her they told her so. Thanks to her lack of a filter even Hannah's own mother would have an opinion that she wouldn't be able to help but share. Naturally, it would be less than flattering. All of which left Hannah in a no-win situation.

Realising she should probably turn around and go home, Hannah couldn't bring herself to do it. Instead, she kept walking. Having a permanently clean house to ramble around in, as her mum put it, continued to be less than fun. As did admiring her treasures.

Hannah missed the noise, the running around here there and everywhere, and even the mess that came with twin teenagers. She wanted to hear her children's jokes, their laughter, and listen to their chatter over dinner. Beth and Archie had been the centre of Hannah's world from the day they were born and despite having looked forward to some well-earned me time, Hannah was lost without them. Reaching a side junction, she stepped off the kerb.

"Watch out!"

Hannah heard a high-pitched screech and before she knew what was happening, she was screaming out as something crashed into her. Losing the grip on her water bottle, it flew out of her hand and into the air, and her feet whipped from beneath her. Everything seemed to move in slow motion as Hannah fell to one side. She yelped in pain as she hit the ground hard.

"Jesus Christ! Are you okay?"

Suddenly a man was upon Hannah and while she tried to right herself, he tried to stop her.

"Stay still," he said. "Something might be broken."

Ignoring his advice, Hannah didn't even look at the man. She simply shrugged him off and hauled herself up into a seating position. Grimacing, she rubbed her ankle, knowing both it and her backside were going to be black and blue thanks to the force with which she'd gone down.

At last, Hannah glanced around at her surroundings. A road bike lay on its side with its wheels spinning and her eyes went from that to the crowd that had begun to form. Hannah felt a mix of confusion and embarrassment. Turning her attention on the man, she took in his bright red cycle helmet. "You hit me?"

"There was nothing I could do. You stepped into the road."

"How fast were you going?"

Crouched at Hannah's side, the man didn't appear to notice his grazed legs and forearms. He seemed more concerned for Hannah than he did for himself.

A look that Hannah couldn't discern flickered across the man's face, as she took in his perfect lips and square jawline. Hannah had obviously died and gone to Heaven. In the living world, the Greek god of cyclists would have just ridden off and left her there on the pavement.

"Never mind that, are you okay?"

His question took Hannah by surprise. She knew she hadn't banged her head and therefore hadn't suffered a concussion, but she couldn't remember the last time someone had asked her that. After the loneliness of the previous few days and having been a source of ridicule amongst her family, Hannah suddenly felt overwhelmed by his kindness. Tears sprung in her eyes. "No," she said. "I'm not." Her lips began to quiver. "I'm a joke. To everyone. I have no life outside of being a mum. All I do is cook and clean and my day job is crap."

Without even a glimpse of a mobile phone camera, Hannah watched the onlookers begin to disperse. Evidently, her domestic life was as boring to them as it was to everyone she knew.

"I'm supposed to be taking part in a sponsored charity race that I don't really want to do, and now I've been run over by a blooming bike. To make matters worse, you're being all nice instead of telling me off for not looking where I was going."

As Hannah began to ugly cry, the man didn't seem to know how to respond. Hannah would've put money on him wishing he was anywhere but there.

"Which means you're probably late for some important appointment. Because everybody but me has places to go and people to see. I'm just the person in the background doing all the dirty work. Except I can't even do that now because Beth and Archie are in the South of France with their father, my oh-so fantastic ex-husband."

Hannah didn't know if it was through a sense of pity or duty simply because he'd hit her with his bike, but the man took off his cycling helmet, and running his hand through this thick black hair, sat down on the ground next to her.

"Sounds like someone's having a bad day," he said.

Hannah turned to him, mid-sniff. "Day? Try week."

She suddenly stopped crying and narrowing her eyes, she studied the man next to her. "It's you," she said. No wonder the man had looked at her funny, she realised. She might not have instantly clocked his identity, but he had hers. "Is this payback for the other night?" she asked, inching away from him. "Did you run me over on purpose?"

CHAPTER 12

*H*annah couldn't believe she was face to face with the man who'd previously collided with her car door. "Well? Did you run me over on purpose?" Eyebrows knitted, she continued to wait for an answer to her question.

The man might not have been smiling, but he had an amused glint in his eye. "No, I didn't."

"It's either that, or you're inordinately clumsy," Hannah said, wondering what he found so funny.

"You stepped out in front of me just then, remember."

"So, you're saying this is all a coincidence?" Hannah threw her arms in the air, indicating first his bike and then the fact they were sat on the pavement. She scoffed. "I mean, what are the odds?"

"That's exactly what I'm saying," the man calmly replied. He nodded to Hannah's ankle. "Shouldn't you be more worried about that?"

Hannah wiggled her foot, tentatively, relieved to find that despite the pain it moved well enough. "It'll be fine. No thanks to you." Wanting to simply get home, she wiped her eyes and nose on the bottom of her T-shirt, before pressing her hands down on the ground and trying to stand. Hannah grimaced as a searing pain shot through her heel and she immediately dropped back down on her bum.

"Here, let me see." Clearly not taking no for an answer, the man moved back into a crouching position. Lifting her foot, he didn't even have to undo the laces of Hannah's trainer, it simply slipped off. He frowned, as if questioning why Hannah would even consider running in unsuitable footwear.

"Honestly, I'm okay. You don't have to…"

The man gave Hannah a silencing look, before taking off her sock. His face was full of concentration and his touch gentle as he manipulated her toes and ankle until he seemed satisfied that all was well. "It might be swollen for a day or two, but I think you'll live."

Hannah's eyes widened. "Which is exactly what I just said."

Tucking Hannah's footwear under his arm, the man got up. He held his hands out for Hannah to take.

She considered his offer for a second and deciding she'd no choice but to trust him, Hannah made sure to avoid any unnecessary pressure on her injury as the man hauled her into a standing position. Glad that she didn't have to crawl home, Hannah felt awkward as she waited for him to bid farewell. She held his gaze as his dark-brown eyes seemed to question her next move and suddenly realising she was still holding his hands, Hannah felt her cheeks redden and she abruptly let go.

"Need a lift?" the man asked, indicating his bike.

"I don't think so." Picturing herself on the back of his bike while he pedalled, her trust didn't extend that far. The man had already hit her, who was to say he wouldn't hit another pedestrian. "How old are we? Twelve?"

"Then I should at least walk you to wherever it is you're going."

"There's no need. I only live around the corner." Hannah indicated the way she'd come. "I'll be there in minutes."

The man glanced up the road. "It's a long way to hop."

Hannah watched him reach down and lift his bike with ease. He hung his cycle helmet on one of the handlebars. Placing one hand on the saddle, he motioned for Hannah to take his other to use as a crutch. However, the man wasn't just tall and handsome, there was no denying his muscular frame underneath the yellow Lycra and as Hannah's gaze automatically moved downwards, his offer suddenly seemed a bit too intimate. Linking arms with him instead, Hannah reluctantly accepted his assistance. "Okay. If you must."

He effortlessly manoeuvred the road bike as he strolled, and she limped, along. "I'm Gabe, by the way. Short for Gabriel. Apparently Mum thought I looked like an angel when I was born. Goodness knows why; I've seen the photos. I blame an overdose of gas and air."

"Hannah." Grimacing thanks to her throbbing ankle, the last thing Hannah was in the mood for was small talk.

They, at last, reached Hannah's front garden and with Gabe's help Hannah hobbled through the gate and up to the house entrance. She saw him frown at her beloved stone lion and while he used it to lean his bike against, she fumbled in her jogging pants pocket for her key. Letting herself in, she allowed Gabe to assist her into the hallway. He might have been a stranger, but by then Hannah was in too much agony to complain.

"In here?" he asked, gesturing to the lounge on his right.

She nodded, thinking it was as good a place as any.

He led Hannah to the sofa and sat her down. Plumping up a couple of cushions he positioned them next to one of the arm rests, before placing a third at the other end. He lifted Hannah's legs and spun her round so that the pair supported her back and the single her injured foot. "Cup of tea while I'm here?" he asked.

Wondering why everyone insisted tea made everything better, including twisted ankles it seemed, Hannah paused before answering. For all she knew, the man before her could be a murderer.

"Don't worry. I won't poison it."

Hannah scowled his way, before looking at her swollen ankle. Doubting she'd be able to feed and water herself for any time soon, she supposed she might as well risk it. "The kitchen is straight down the hall," she replied, before watching him exit the room.

Listening to Gabe bang about searching for cups and a spoon, it felt weird having a grown man in the house, let alone one Hannah didn't know. Then again, as she pictured his muscular arms and firm grip as he reached into the top cupboard for the box of teabags, she supposed it wasn't all bad. She did have a handsome chap making her a cuppa. She envisaged his strong thighs brushing again the base units as he poured boiling water into her cup and she sighed. "Enjoy having someone run around after you while it lasts," Hannah told herself, aware he'd soon be gone, never to be seen again.

Gabe reappeared with a steaming mug. "I've put in plenty of sugar."

Despite hating sweet tea, Hannah tried to hide her distaste as he handed it over. However, she clearly didn't hide it well enough.

"You've just had a shock," he said, nodding for her to drink whether she wanted to or not.

Hannah took a sip as instructed, while Gabe sat down on the sofa arm at her feet.

"Is there anyone I can call?" he asked. "To come and look after you?"

Hannah was about to tell him there was no one when she suddenly heard the front door opening. Not expecting any visitors, she cocked her head wondering who was there.

"It's only me," her guest called out.

Hannah looked to Gabe in all his Lycra glory and knowing the voice belonged to her mother, felt a slight panic. Janice's response to her daughter being hit by a cyclist while out jogging, Hannah could cope with. Her mum coming across the Greek God of Cycling in her living room, not so much.

Hannah cringed, recalling every embarrassing moment she'd experienced at the hands of her mum. Whenever Hannah found herself within two feet of a man, Janice mentally booked a wedding and chose names for her non-existent grandchildren. Hannah threw her head back against the cushions. As if her morning hadn't been bad enough.

CHAPTER 13

"*H*annah, you do know there's a road bike leaning against your…" Appearing in the lounge doorway, Janice fell silent. A sensual pout crossed her lips, and she raised her hand and preened her hair. "When we spoke earlier you didn't mention you were expecting company." Janice might have been talking to Hannah, but her eyes didn't leave Gabe.

"Because I wasn't," Hannah replied.

A tall thin elderly woman appeared right behind Janice. "Oh my," she said, also spotting Gabe.

Hannah almost didn't recognise Aunt Dorothy. Yes, it had been a while since she'd seen her, but Dorothy had lost a tonne of weight and her smile didn't appear quite as bright. She carried an old-fashioned suitcase in one hand and much to Hannah's confusion, what looked like a fancy ginger jar in the other. Decorated in a delicate green floral design, Hannah supposed at least it was pretty.

"You didn't tell me she had a boyfriend," Dorothy said.

"I didn't *know* she had a boyfriend," Janice said.

Hannah rolled her eyes. "That's because I don't."

"Then pray tell who this handsome chap is," Janice asked.

"Yes, please do," Dorothy said.

Hannah understood why the two women were so enamoured. Gabe might be a walking accident but he was gorgeous with it.

Gabe rose to his feet. "I'm Gabe." With his arm outstretched, he shook Hannah's Mum's hand.

"Janice," Janice replied, coming over all coy.

Gabe turned his attention to Hannah's aunt.

"Dorothy," she said, equally charmed.

With their gaze firmly on Gabe and his yellow Lycra, Hannah squirmed wishing the man had done a proper job of running her over. If he had, she'd be in a hospital, in a coma, oblivious to her mum and Dorothy's desperate behaviour.

"I should go," Gabe said.

Although glad to hear it, Hannah couldn't blame him for wanting to leave. As first impressions went, she supposed as a family, they'd proved themselves a treat.

"Not on our account, I hope," Mum said.

Who else's? Hannah thought.

Gabe turned his attention to Hannah. "Take care of that ankle, yeah?"

She nodded.

"And please get some trainers that fit."

As far as Hannah was concerned, she didn't need to. Her running days were over. She fixed Gabe with a smile. "While we're dishing out advice, you might want to get your eyes tested."

"What are you talking about? What's happened to her ankle?" Janice asked.

Hannah shook her head in despair. If her mum hadn't been ogling, she'd have noticed Hannah's injured foot for herself. "I tripped and fell."

"While you were out jogging, I suppose?" Janice sniffed. "If God wanted us to run, he'd have made us all as fit as your boyfriend here."

"Again, he's not my boyfriend."

Janice ignored Hannah. "Isn't that right, Gabe?"

Moving to leave, he clearly found the situation funny.

It was the first time Hannah had seen him properly smile. If he was handsome when he was annoyed, he was even more lovely when he wasn't.

"Nice to meet you, ladies," he said. Giving Hannah a parting wink, Gabe made his exit.

Janice and Dorothy craned their necks to watch him go, leaving Hannah unable to believe what she was seeing.

As soon as the front door closed behind Gabe, Janice turned to Hannah with a smirk.

"Well, well, well. Aren't you the dark horse."

"Curb your enthusiasm, Mother," Hannah said. "I've already told you things aren't what you think."

Janice's face fell. "They're not what I'd hoped, you mean." She sighed. "I should have known it was too good to be true."

"Yes, you should." Hannah snickered to herself, remembering the time Janice assumed the chap from the electricity board was Hannah's new suitor. The poor man had only called to read the meter. While on another occasion Janice mistook the window cleaner for a person of interest. Anyone else and the fact that he carried a squeegee and was at the kitchen sink filling up a bucket of water would have been clue enough.

"Before you say it," Janice said, as if reading Hannah's mind. "I'm not the only one to have thought window cleaners were a thing of the past." With a wounded expression, she turned to Dorothy. "Am I so wrong for wanting my daughter to experience even a smidgen of happiness?" She looked back at Hannah. "No one's trying to marry you off. It's called getting out there and enjoying yourself once in a while."

"I do have fun as a single woman, you know."

"Really?" Janice said. "I can't say I've noticed."

Janice had made it clear that she hated Hannah's single status. She seemed convinced that if she didn't do something about it,

Hannah would end up with a house full of cats in her dotage. Hannah opened her mouth to defend herself, but Janice shut her down.

"And please don't give me that rubbish about being too busy caring for Beth and Archie to even think about having a life. The twins are practically adults."

Hannah looked at her mum, aghast. "They're *fifteen*."

"Exactly! They'll be off to university in a couple of years or so." Janice scoffed. "What excuse will you come up with then?"

Hannah threw her head back against the sofa arm. "I give up."

"Believe me, you did that a long time ago." Janice returned her attention to Hannah's aunt. "Now, where do you want Denis?"

Hannah's head shot back up. "You mean that's…?"

"Your uncle, yes. Who else would it be?" Janice glanced around the room as if what she was doing was perfectly normal. "On the mantelpiece, Dorothy? Or at the window so he can watch the world go by?"

Dorothy handed over the ginger jar. "On the mantel for now, I think."

Except it wasn't a ginger jar at all and as Janice gave it pride of place above the fire, Hannah recoiled at the thought of having a dead man's ashes in her living room.

"Now, let me show you where you'll be sleeping," Janice said, indicating she and Dorothy head upstairs to the spare room.

As the two women disappeared, Hannah grumbled to herself on the sofa. As much as it would be nice to catch up with her aunt, that didn't negate Hannah and her mum's prior conversation. When she'd said no to having a house guest, Hannah had meant it and she couldn't believe her mum had brought her over regardless.

Hannah wanted to call them back into the lounge, to tell her mum that as per their discussion, Dorothy would have to find alternative sleeping arrangements. Hannah took a deep breath to suppress her frustration, knowing it wasn't her aunt's fault that Janice had a hearing problem when it suited.

Hannah stared at her swollen ankle for a moment, before reaching into her pocket and pulling out her phone. From a foot injury to an unsolicited house guest, to say the day wasn't panning out quite like Hannah had planned was an understatement. Typing in a message and firing it off to Mel and Liv, Hannah knew pulling out of the sponsored run was the right thing to do and she scolded herself for acting on impulse in the first place, rather than thinking things through.

Hannah suddenly felt as if someone was watching her and with no one else in the room, her eyes were drawn to Uncle Denis on the mantel. His presence made her feel increasingly uncomfortable. Awkward even, as if she should be talking to him. Needing to do something to break the silence, Hannah opened her mouth to speak, almost jumping off the sofa when heavy footsteps on the stairs beat her to it.

"I've left your aunt unpacking her things," Janice said, re-entering the lounge. She paused. "Hannah, are you okay?"

"I'm fine." No way was she telling her mum the urn gave her the heebie-jeebies.

Janice narrowed her eyes as if not quite believing her. She shook herself out of it. "It's time I got back to the builders. Is there anything you need before I go?" Janice nodded to the cold mug of tea Hannah held. "Another cup? Or shall I just leave you in Aunt Dorothy's capable hands?"

Hannah scowled at the situation her mum had put her in.

"Hannah, please don't sulk. It's not becoming of a grown woman."

"I'm not sulking. This is my annoyed face." Hannah kept her voice low. "I don't mean to be awful, but I told you not to bring Aunt Dorothy here."

"From what I can see it's a good job I did." Janice gestured to Hannah's foot. "You clearly need someone to look after you." She leaned down and kissed the top of Hannah's head. "You're always running around after everyone else. Enjoy being the recipient for a change. Lord knows you deserve it." Moving to leave, Janice stopped in the doorway. "While we're on the subject of what you deserve, Hannah, not every man's like Carl."

"I do know that, Mum."

"No, love. You don't."

CHAPTER 14

THREE WEEKS UNTIL RACE DAY

*G*abe grimaced. After colliding with Hannah and coming off his bike, he must have hit the ground harder than he'd thought. He'd felt nothing at the time, probably because his adrenalin had kicked in the second he realised he was about to hit someone, only to increase all over again when he realised who that someone was. A couple of days later, however, and his whole being had begun to ache. He laughed. Maybe Hannah was right when she'd said he needed glasses.

His body stiff and steps tentative, Gabe finished showering, got dressed, and made his way downstairs to the kitchen.

"Looks like someone's overdone things on the exercise front," Roger said, seeing Gabe struggle.

Gabe snorted. "If only."

"Here, sit down." Roger pulled a chair out from the table. Frowning, he indicated Gabe's wounded forearms. "They look nasty."

Gabe glanced down at the brown cuts and abrasions on his skin. Caused by friction when his arms had scraped against the pavement, the result looked worse than it felt. "They're just grazes."

Roger headed straight for the kettle. "Let me make you some tea."

Gabe chuckled. Tea, the solution to all life's problems.

"What happened?" Roger asked, as he filled the kettle and grabbed mugs from the cupboard.

"I came off my bike the other day."

"That's not like you."

"A woman stepped out in front of me."

Roger spun round to face Gabe.

"Don't worry. She's fine. Apart from a twisted ankle." He watched Roger shudder, as if feeling the pain. "It was as much my fault though." Gabe glanced over at the white envelope. Having slung it on the kitchen counter the day it had been delivered, it had lain there ever since. "I wasn't concentrating properly."

Roger followed Gabe's gaze.

"I'll read it when I'm ready," Gabe said, knowing exactly what his dad was thinking.

Roger shrugged. "Nothing to do with me." He got back to making the tea.

Gabe considered his collision with Hannah. The fear in her face as she had tumbled to the ground had sent a panic straight through him. Her subsequent meltdown when he'd asked if she was okay confused him. And her utter shock when she, at last, recognised Gabe made him secretly laugh. Not only had Gabe clocked Hannah's identity from the off, he'd never been accused of attempted murder before.

Despite being in agony, Hannah was as feisty then as she'd been the first time Gabe had met her. A characteristic she'd obviously inherited from her mother. Recalling how Janice *and* Dorothy had greeted him, the women in that family weren't exactly reserved.

Roger placed a mug of tea in front of Gabe. "What's so funny?"

Gabe hadn't realised he was smiling. Then again, he found it hard not to when it came to Hannah. Gabe didn't just find her amusing; he found her intriguing. "Nothing," he said.

"So, did you call an ambulance? To make sure she was checked over properly?" Taking the seat opposite, Roger wrapped his hands around his cup. "Looking at the state of you, I can only imagine the condition *she* must be in."

"No, but I made sure she got home. It wasn't far. Just off the high street. You'll probably know the house. It's the one with that giant ugly lion at the door."

"Oh, yes." Roger said. "Lots of blonde hair."

"Dad, it's not wearing a wig. It's a stone statue."

"Not the lion." Roger sniggered. "The woman who owns it. I see her coming and going sometimes with her two kids. On my way to the cemetery to visit your mum. Pretty young thing. Friendly."

Gabe let out a laugh. "You think?" Stubborn, argumentative, accusatory… of all the descriptions Gabe could have used to describe Hannah, friendly was not one of them.

"She's always been nice to me. I mean, I've never had a conversation with the woman. But I've said hello, which she always returns with a *hi* or a little wave. Then again, I've never run her over either." He thought for a moment. "I don't suppose you know what she's called, do you?"

"Her name's Hannah. Why?"

"No reason. Other than the fact that it's nice to put a name to a pretty face."

Gabe might not view Hannah as friendly like his dad did, but he certainly agreed she was pretty. He suddenly felt Roger's eyes on him. "What?"

"You're doing it again."

"Doing what?"

"Smiling."

"And that's a crime now, is it?"

"No, but it *is* interesting." Roger sipped on his tea. "I can't remember the last time you did that over a woman."

CHAPTER 15

*H*annah stirred and not wanting to wake from the best of dreams, she clung on to an image of Gabe. He'd just returned from a meeting with his fellow Olympian gods and unable to deny his love for Hannah any longer, was determined to make his feelings known. He threw off his himation, refusing to hide his heart any longer. The last thing Gabe wanted was a cloak preventing Hannah from seeing where his lay. Standing there in only his chiton, Hannah ran her fingers across his bare shoulder and well-defined pectoralis major. At the feel of her touch, Gabe got down on bended knee...

The sound of banging and clattering filtered into Hannah's brain and Gabe faded into black. Hannah properly awoke and opening her eyes, her mind flitted between disappointment and confusion.

Realising Aunt Dorothy was responsible for the commotion, Hannah breathed the aroma of herbs and spices. She shot up in bed. Those weren't breakfast smells and grabbing her phone off the bedside table, she frantically questioned just how long she'd slept. Relieved it was only 9.30am, she threw herself back against her pillow. Although a lie-in for her, it could have been far worse.

Laying there, she supposed she should get up and flipping the duvet over to one side, swung her legs off the bed. As her feet hit the ground she cocked her head, pleased to note her foot was almost pain free. Again, thanks to Dorothy, Hannah acknowledged.

Hannah couldn't deny her gratitude as she recalled the care Dorothy had provided since the road bike incident. As soon as Janice had left them to it, Dorothy had swung into action and insisted on an ice pack for Hannah's swollen ankle. Unable to find one, or indeed any frozen peas, she'd utilised what was in the freezer and produced a bag of frozen chips. Dorothy had been playing nurse extraordinaire ever since.

Putting on her dressing gown, Hannah stuffed her phone into one of the pockets and headed downstairs. At the same time appreciating how wonderful it had been to be taken care of, instead of doing the caring, for a change. Not that it had been an easy transition. It had always been Hannah's job to make sure everyone else had everything they needed and handing over that responsibility felt akin to making herself redundant.

As she neared the kitchen, her ears pricked at the sound of Dorothy talking and wondering who to, Hannah stopped to listen.

"I'd forgotten how much I love cooking," Dorothy said. "I know, I know, I could easily do this at home. But nothing tastes the same without you there to enjoy it with me."

Hannah's heart went out to her aunt. The woman was obviously talking to Uncle Denis.

"And microwave meals aren't so bad once you get used to them."

Hannah pictured her aunt sat in a cold soulless kitchen. Spoon in hand, Dorothy looked down at a plate of watery ready-made beef stew. Hannah sighed. That was no life for anyone.

"Don't worry. I'm not going to get all morbid on you. Not today." Dorothy exhaled a happy sigh. "I'm enjoying myself too much. I can't tell you how good it is to feel useful again." She paused. "You should've seen that poor girl's foot. I did what I could, but you never know with ankle injuries. I have a feeling I might be here for a while."

Hearing the hope in Dorothy's voice brought a lump to Hannah's throat.

"And to have someone to properly chat to is wonderful. No offence, Denis. You're a great listener, but you have to agree conversations are better when they're two-way."

Hannah looked down at her foot. The swelling had gone, and the pain was nowhere near what it was, but having heard what she'd just heard, she couldn't let Dorothy know that. Hannah took a few steps back and practised a limp. Hoping it looked genuine, she coughed to signal her arrival as she entered the kitchen.

Hannah couldn't believe the sight that met her, and her eyes widened. "Someone's been busy." Mountains of chopped vegetables sat on the kitchen worktop and pans of ingredients boiled on the stove. A meat joint roasted in the oven and rolled out pastry lay in a baking tray awaiting its filling. Hannah's mouth watered at the delectable smells floating on the air. "I'm impressed."

Stood at the stove stirring, Dorothy looked Hannah's way. "I thought a spot of batch cooking was in order."

Hannah let out a laugh. "A spot? It's like a factory production line in here."

Dorothy grinned. "I hope you don't mind, but you had so much food, it would've been a shame to let it go to waste."

Hannah thought back to her unnecessary shopping trip. Tossing things willy-nilly into her trolley, she hadn't thought to check sell-by dates. "I did go a bit overboard at the supermarket."

"Shopping for one does take a little getting used to. The money I wasted when Denis first…" Dorothy's voice trailed off and a sadness crossed her face. However, as quickly as it had appeared it was gone, and she fixed another smile on her lips. "Tea? Coffee?" she asked, turning her attention to the kettle.

"Here, let me." Hannah limped forward to intervene. "Your hands are already full with all this." She indicated Dorothy's food prep.

"You'll do no such thing. You sit down. Rest your foot."

As Hannah sat down at the table, her eyes were drawn to Uncle Denis's urn. He and Aunt Dorothy hadn't only been married for over fifty years, they'd been inseparable. For Dorothy, losing him must have been like losing a part of herself and Hannah could only imagine how lonely the woman must feel.

"I bet you think I'm mad for bringing him with me," Dorothy said, following Hannah's gaze.

"Not at all," Hannah replied. Although if her aunt had asked her that prior to her eavesdropping she'd have had to say yes.

"And, no doubt, you heard me talking to him just then, which *must* make you think I'm barmy."

Hannah felt herself blush. It was wrong of her to listen in.

"Don't worry. I sometimes wonder if I'm losing it myself." Handing Hannah her drink, Dorothy took the seat opposite. "You were limping on the wrong foot just now, by the way."

Embarrassed, Hannah opened her mouth to explain, but Dorothy started talking again before she got the chance.

"When a partner dies, it's not just your best friend you lose, it's life as you've always known it. Be it your day-to-day routine, social settings, or even what you'd normally watch on television, that one death impacts on everything." Dorothy sighed. "A bit like you at the supermarket, I suppose, doing a monthly shop for three. You knew Beth and Archie weren't going to be here to eat any of it, but it's automatic. You buy what you always buy because that's the way it's always been. You don't have to think about it, it's in your psyche."

Hannah fully understood where Dorothy was coming from.

"So, as you can imagine, when Denis died, not only was I dealing with the loss of someone I loved, I also had to unlearn the simplest of tasks, if that makes sense."

Hannah reached out with a comforting hand. "It does."

"I'm sure there are those who expect me to get over it. As if there's a time limit on grieving and at some point, I should just snap out of it. If only it was that easy, eh? I can't tell you how mad I am at Denis for not letting me go first."

Hannah sympathised. "I'm sure no one expects you to snap out of anything, Aunt Dorothy."

"When he first passed. I hardly got a minute to myself. I had to organise his send-off which meant lots of dealings with the undertaker and whatnot. Everyone rallied round. Friends and neighbours were always checking in on me and the phone didn't stop ringing with people offering their condolences." She sipped her tea. "Then came the day of the funeral." She became pensive for a moment as if picturing it. "After that people stopped coming."

Thinking about it, Hannah supposed funerals were a sort of closure. Yes, everyone grieved differently but funerals gave mourners the opportunity to say goodbye to their loved ones and ultimately, gain a sense of acceptance. However, while this enabled many people to move on in the grieving process, Hannah supposed it meant those like Dorothy suddenly found themselves isolated. "That must have been difficult," Hannah said.

"Don't get me wrong, I understood why. Life goes on, as they say. And the last thing I wanted was to be a burden. But to go from everyone to no one. It was hard. Of course, that left me with the choice of either talking to the walls or talking to Denis. I've always been chatty, Hannah." Dorothy glanced over at Denis's urn. "And thanks to that green pot, I still can be."

"I understand. And please, you carry on with your chatting... to me and Denis. And also know, not only are you welcome here for as long as you like, after hurting my foot, I don't know what I'd have done without you."

"You'd have managed."

"I would. But it's been nice not having to for once."

A sudden loud knock at the front door interrupted their conversation and Hannah looked to Dorothy, surprised. "It's a bit early for visitors, don't you think?"

CHAPTER 16

*L*eaving Aunt Dorothy at the table, Hannah got up from her seat and went to answer the door. Her eyes widened when she saw a delivery woman standing there with a huge bouquet of flowers. Made up of a summery cocktail of pink roses, purple alliums, magenta germini, and pink phlox, it was finished with purple mint and soft pink berries.

The delivery woman gave Hannah a huge smile. "Someone's a lucky girl," she said, handing them over.

Hannah tried to tell her she must have the wrong address, but before she could get the words out, the delivery woman was back at her van and climbing in.

Hannah searched the flora and fauna for a card and pulling it free saw her name written on the little envelope. *Strange*, she thought. *It's not my birthday.* She let out a little squeal. *Then again, even if it was, no one would ever think to send me flowers.*

Intrigued as to who had sent them, Hannah carried them into the kitchen and placed them on the table.

"Special occasion or special someone?" Dorothy asked.

As Hannah opened the envelope and read the message, her pulse quickened. A dreamy image of Gabe, wearing nothing but his chiton as he prepared to declare his undying love for her, sprang into Hannah's head. She looked to Dorothy. "Neither." She swallowed hard. "They're from Gabe. You know, the cyclist who ran into me."

"Once seen never forgotten," Dorothy said, followed by a naughty laugh. "Wouldn't you say?"

Unable to disagree, Hannah would say that, but didn't.

"Is there a telephone number included?"

Hannah's pulse sped up even more as she stared at the digits. As far as she was concerned, men as good looking as Gabe could have any woman they wanted and ergo, weren't usually in the habit of pursuing single mothers of teenage children. "Nope." Insisting the flowers were simply an apology, Hannah slipped the card into her pocket. "Just his name."

Dorothy's shoulders slumped.

Hannah hated lying to her aunt, but she knew if she told Dorothy the truth, she'd only keep on until Hannah rang the number. Besides, it was probably only there because the florist had mistakenly added it.

Hannah's phone suddenly vibrated in her pocket. Pulling it out, Beth's name flashed up. "It's the kids." Her eyes brightened. "Two surprises in one day and it's not even 11am." She looked to Dorothy. "Do you mind if I take it?"

"Of course not." Dorothy picked up the bouquet of flowers. "You go ahead. I'll find something to put these in."

CHAPTER 17

$\mathcal{L}$eaving Aunt Dorothy to her cooking, Hannah clicked to answer Beth and Archie's call as she made her way into the lounge.

Their gleeful faces appeared on screen. "Hi, Mum," they both said.

Hannah balanced her phone against the coffee table bowl. "Hello, you two." Pleased to see them looking well, she settled herself on the sofa. "Still having a good time?"

"Are we," Beth said. "We're off to Saint-Tropez shortly. Specifically..." She paused as if for effect. "Pampelonne beach."

Her daughter obviously had a desired response in mind and Hannah dipped her chin accordingly, indicating she was impressed.

"It's where all the Hollywood stars go to relax," Beth carried on. "Renowned artists too, but I'm not sure I'd recognise them."

Hannah envisaged the South of France's picturesque coastline, with its golden beaches and turquoise sea. "It's all right for some."

"While she's celebrity spotting, I'm gonna to do some

snorkelling," Archie said. "And before you ask, yes, I *am* wearing sun lotion."

"I can see that," Hannah said. "You'd be like a peeling lobster otherwise."

"Did you know Saint-Tropez is named after a roman officer called Torpes?" Beth asked. "I read all about it in Monica's travel guide come history book."

"Glad to hear you're developing your knowledge as well as your tan," Hannah said, astonished to hear it.

"He worked under the Emperor Nero. At least he did until Nero had him decapitated for converting to Christianity."

"And his body was put on a small boat and pushed out to sea," Hannah added. "In Pisa, as I recall. Only to land on the shores of what we now know as Saint-Tropez."

Beth and Archie looked back at Hannah, confused.

"Where do you even learn these things?" Archie asked. Screwing up his face, he obviously remembered their last conversation when Hannah mentioned *La bise.*

Recalling it too, Hannah wondered if her children had always thought her uninformed, or if that was a recent development. Tempted to ask them, her attention was diverted when Dorothy popped her head through the lounge doorway.

"Sorry to interrupt. But I've brought you a fresh cup of tea."

"Thank you," Hannah said, as her aunt tiptoed in and placed it on the coffee table. "Aunt Dorothy, say hello to Beth and Archie, my children."

Evidently not used to video calls, Dorothy froze as she looked at them. "Hello," she said. Standing there like a stunned mullet, she spoke without moving her lips.

"Hello," Beth and Archie replied. Clearly asking themselves who the strange woman in their living room was, they couldn't seem to think of anything else to say.

As Hannah looked from the screen to her aunt and back again, the silence between the three of them was deafening.

Dorothy turned her attention back to Hannah. "I'll leave you to it," she said, tiptoeing out again.

"Who was that?" Beth asked.

Archie appeared equally bemused. "And what's she doing in our house?"

"Aunt Dorothy's your granddad's cousin. I used to spend my summer holidays in Norfolk with her and Uncle Denis."

Beth and Archie looked back at Hannah, evidently none the wiser.

"Uncle Denis died a little while ago. I couldn't attend his funeral because you were both sick, remember?"

They obviously didn't.

"Never mind," Hannah said, a tad disappointed in their joint memory lapse. "She'll probably be back in Norfolk by the time you land home anyway."

"Time to go," Carl called through. "Beth! Archie!"

Hannah frowned at the sound of his voice. "Isn't he coming to say hello?"

"He's avoiding you," Beth said.

"Why?"

Beth and Archie blushed and shifting in their seats, they no longer looked directly at their screen.

"Is everything all right?" Worried, Hannah refused to let worst-case scenarios take hold of her mind. "Has something happened?"

"Everything's fine," Beth said.

She and Archie didn't look fine.

Beth fidgeted some more. "Apart from us needing to say sorry."

"It's why we rang," Archie said.

Hannah narrowed her eyes. "Sorry about what?"

"For the other day," Beth said.

Archie played with his hands. "We shouldn't have laughed at you over the sponsored run."

Hannah told herself she must have stepped into the twilight zone. Her children weren't in the habit of apologising for anything, and watching them squirm, she silently questioned where their need to start stemmed from.

As if reading Hannah's mind, Beth rolled her eyes in typical teenager fashion. "Monica had a word. And not just with us. She told Dad off for his behaviour too."

Hannah pictured Carl getting a scolding and knowing he'd have hated every second of it, tried not to smirk. No wonder he was staying out of the way. He probably didn't think he'd done anything to apologise for.

"She said Dad was lucky to have an ex-wife like you. If she were in your shoes, no way would *she* be so understanding," Archie said.

"Monica thinks we should have all been more supportive. Instead of being disrespectful," Beth said.

As a mum, Hannah felt uncomfortable at someone else admonishing her children. At the same time, the more she heard about Carl's girlfriend, the more Hannah liked her.

"And what do you two you think?" The impression Beth and Archie had given thus far, suggested they were saying sorry purely because they'd been instructed to.

"That she's right," Beth said. "We were wrong to react the way we did."

"And when we said you don't do anything, we didn't mean anything at all," Archie added. "We know you work hard. For us and at your job."

"We were just surprised."

"Because you pretty much only ever do stuff that involves us."

Hannah sighed, irritated to hear her children echo the sentiments made clear by Mel, Liv, and Hannah's mum. They were all correct in their assertions, of course. The fact that Hannah was bereft when Beth and Archie had left for France proved that. As did the spotless house she sat in and Dorothy's batch cooking thanks to Hannah's excessive supermarket spree. Hannah just wished people would stop mentioning it.

"Anyway, we've decided we want to sponsor you," Beth said.

"A month's spending money. From each of us," Archie said.

"Dad's gonna throw a big wad in too."

"And we all want you to know how proud we are of you for doing it."

"It's only a charity run," Hannah said. Yes, she'd previously hoped for some encouragement over the race, but with talk of pride and large sums of cash it seemed they were taking things to the extreme. Seeing their earnestness, Hannah felt embarrassed. She didn't have a clue how to tell them she'd pulled out of the event altogether.

"Beth! Archie!" Carl called out, thankfully saving Hannah from having to explain. "Two minutes and we're leaving, with or without you."

Hannah frowned at Carl's tone. He sounded weary. "Your dad is okay, isn't he?"

"Apart from nagging us not to get sand in the house," Beth said.

"And to hang our towels out to dry after being in the pool," Archie said.

"And to put our plates in the dishwasher after we've eaten."

"And to stop bickering when we annoy each other."

Hannah smiled. It had only been a week and it seemed Carl was already well acquainted with the delights of full-time parenting. "Tell Dad welcome to my world."

"We should go," Beth said.

Hannah wished they didn't have to. "Have fun and say hello to Torpes for me," she said, regardless. "You'll find a statue of him erected in an alcove on the façade of the Church Notre-Dame-de-L'Assomption de Saint-Tropez."

Beth and Archie looked from her to each other, but before

they could ask how she'd know that Hannah gave them a wave, a quick "bye", and ended the call.

She sat in the silence for a moment. Relishing in the fact that Hannah's children had never told her they were proud of her before, she felt a bit choked.

Hannah looked down at her injured foot, wanting nothing more than for Beth and Archie's pride to continue. But while the pain she'd suffered had abated, she knew that didn't necessarily mean her ankle was strong enough to run on. Even if Hannah told Mel and Liv she was back in the race, there was no guarantee she'd finish. And if she didn't, what would Beth and Archie think of her then?

Picking up her phone Hannah typed in a message. Staring at it for a moment, she was tempted to press delete. "Sod it," Hannah said and in a now-or-never moment, pressed send.

Re: the race. I'm in. Again!

CHAPTER 18

*S*tood upright on his pedals, Gabe gripped his handlebars and used his body weight to control his bike. He needed as much stability as he could get to negotiate the rough terrain of the craggy mountainside. Hyped up on adrenalin, Gabe's concentration was acute as he made the steep descent. Navigating narrow ridges, rocks and unpredictable scree was a dangerous business. One wrong move and Gabe knew both he and his bike could be tumbling into the vertical distance.

It felt exhilarating to be in the great outdoors. Gabe's mind had been clouded of late, and the challenge presented by his current environment, combined with glorious sunshine and lungs full of fresh air, was just what he needed.

Gabe heard Slim's tyres slipping and sliding behind him, and eventually a triumphant howl as Slim celebrated the fact they'd, at last, reached the bottom. Hitting his brakes, Gabe angled his bike almost side on as he fast brought it to a standstill and within seconds, Slim was doing the same.

Dismounting, Gabe took off his helmet and tossed it to one side. Unbuckling his rucksack, he swung it off his back. He flopped to the ground, while Slim checked his smartwatch.

"Brilliant. We're up," he said, evidently chuffed with their improved performance. Sitting down next to Gabe, Slim guzzled on his water bottle.

Gabe unzipped his bag and took out a water bottle of his own. Uncapping its lid, he drank long and hard. Thirst quenched, he reached into his bag for a second time and producing a hand towel, used it to wipe his forehead. He took off his cycle top to further cool down, enjoying the feel of the breeze as it blew against his skin.

"What happened to you?" Slim asked, clocking Gabe's grazes.

"I rode into someone and ended up in a heap on the tarmac."

"Bloody hell." Slim laughed. "I dread to think what state your target's in."

"Target!" Gabe laughed too. "I wasn't *aiming* for her. She ended up with a twisted ankle and probably a few bruises."

"She? Oh, mate."

"Tell me about it." Gabe fell quiet, not sure if he should mention his accident was more awkward than Slim thought. That the other party concerned was car door woman.

"What?" Furrowing his brow, Slim was evidently onto him. He waited for Gabe to answer.

Gabe relented. "It was her again."

Slim thought for a second, before realisation seemed to dawn. "The one who hit you with–"

"Yep," Gabe interrupted.

Slim let out a laugh.

"You can't make it up, can you?"

Slim appeared impressed. "What are the chances of that?" He stared at Gabe wide-eyed. "I think someone's trying to tell you something here."

Gabe scoffed. Serendipity, divine intervention, kismet, fate… Slim could call it what he liked. Gabe didn't believe in any of it. "You mean I need to pay more attention to my surroundings?"

"I'm telling you. Twice in one week. Something cosmic's going on." Slim looked at Gabe with a grin. "If you see her again, you should ask her out."

CHAPTER 19

*H*annah had spent the previous couple of days testing her injured foot. However, rather than meander aimlessly, she'd come up with a simple circular route that was flat and easily timed. Her walk might not have stretched to 5k like in the sponsored run, and it certainly wasn't as challenging as Wethersham Hall's woodland, but it was enough to see if Hannah's ankle held out. She'd even treated herself to some new trainers. A proper assessment wouldn't have been possible if her feet were sliding about in Beth's old pair.

That day, as she neared the top of the high street on her return leg, Hannah was surprised at how easily she'd got into the routine of walking. Striding along, she'd begun to enjoy it. It felt good to get out into the sunshine and clear her head. Hannah might not be on target to win records like Mel had done, but there were other benefits. One, she was getting regular exercise and two, she was able to sort through the worries that had snuck into her brain of late.

She scoffed as she walked. Beth and Archie's trip to France had meant to be a break for her too; a chance to have some proper down time for once. But from the second her children had left the last thing Hannah had done was relax. Instead, she'd found herself in a constant emotional quandary, as if forces were conspiring to make her think about her life in a way she hadn't considered before.

As she stepped aside for a young woman with a pram, Hannah couldn't help but take note. Even that felt symbolic. Yet another message to remind her that her existence solely revolved around Beth and Archie and as much then as it had when they were babies.

Of course, Aunt Dorothy's arrival hadn't helped. Her aunt's loneliness had struck a chord. All thanks to Janice, who'd pointed out it wouldn't be too long until Beth and Archie were off to university. Her mum was right to mention it though. If Hannah couldn't cope with them being away for a month, how would she manage when that time came?

Hannah pictured Dorothy's solitary existence down in Norfolk. Like her, if Hannah didn't act would she too be sat in a soulless kitchen staring down at a ready-made meal for one? While her children were off studying and partying to their hearts' content.

"Hannah!" a voice called out.

Coming from the other side of the road, she glanced over to see Gabe on his bike. Hannah's face fell and she willed him to stay put. Feeling hot and sweaty thanks to her vigorous walk, she knew if he got too close, he'd wish he hadn't given her his number. Not that she planned on ringing it anyway, she reminded herself.

She watched him check for traffic and pedal in her direction regardless and cringing at the state of herself, she swiped away the hair that had stuck to her forehead and forced herself to smile.

"Big improvement with your ankle, I see." Bringing his bike to a standstill, Gabe climbed off.

Hannah looked down at her foot. "So far, so good." As Gabe

took off his helmet and ran his hands through his locks, Hannah almost swooned. Between them they looked like stars of a shampoo ad, with her as the before, and him the after.

"Glad to see you took my advice and picked up some new trainers."

Hannah blushed, recalling their last meeting. Wearing oversized footwear probably contributed to her hitting the ground the way she had. From the whole sorry collision to her ugly crying, to Mum and Aunt Dorothy's ogling, it was a day she wanted to forget. But there Gabe was reminding her. "Not that you took mine," Hannah said. "Or are you wearing contact lenses?"

As Gabe threw his head back and laughed, Hannah found his confidence unnerving. She didn't know why. After all, she was used to dealing with Carl. Not that that was a fair comparison, Hannah realised. There was a fine line between self-assurance and arrogance; the latter was something her ex-husband was full of.

"Thank you for the flowers, by the way," Hannah said. He might not have brought them up, but she thought she should. "They were completely unnecessary."

"Flowers?" Gabe frowned at Hannah for a moment, as if she'd said something wrong.

Hannah frowned at Gabe in return, wondering what his problem was. In her view, why bother sending someone a bouquet if they're not supposed to mention it? She sniffed. Why include a telephone number?

"Yes. The flowers. Sorry." Gabe seemed to gather himself. He gestured to the café a few doors up. "Erm, fancy a coffee?"

A voice inside of Hannah screamed yes, most definitely. The man was a Greek god. However, Hannah found herself hesitating, as another voice warned her to stay well away. The man was a player. Besides, it further insisted, Dorothy waiting, stop clock at the ready.

Hannah knew Dorothy wouldn't really mind. If anything, she'd be delighted by the fact that Hannah had bumped into Gabe again. Moreover, she'd be ecstatic to learn Hannah had socialised with the man.

"My treat," Gabe said, eyebrow raised.

Taking in Gabe's anticipation, butterflies fluttered in Hannah's tummy. A sensation of nerves and excitement, she'd long forgotten what that felt like. A Hellenic deity had never asked Hannah to join them for a drink before and having spent that morning's walk mulling over her life, Hannah knew it was about time she did something out of the ordinary.

She took a deep breath ready to accept his invitation.

"Maybe some other time," she said. "Aunt Dorothy will be worried if I'm not back soon."

CHAPTER 20

Making his way home, Gabe wished he'd ignored Slim's advice regarding Hannah. If he had, he wouldn't feel so stupid after she'd just turned him down. Of course she wouldn't want to join him for coffee. What would they have talked about? They were opposites. Sports were his thing, while she was, no doubt, bookish.

Lost in his own thoughts, Gabe suddenly jumped at the sound of a car beeping. Gripping his handlebars, he struggled to stop his bike from careering up the kerb and onto the pavement. Gabe was used to vehicles getting too close as they overtook, but with his mind elsewhere Gabe hadn't noticed that day's boy racer. "Idiot!" Gabe shouted as the car driver carried on up the road.

Righting his bike, Gabe was more frustrated with himself than anyone else. Ever since he'd first met Hannah, she seemed to have made herself at home in his head and had no intention of leaving. He'd tried to kick her out, of course, but she refused to hand over her key and kept moving back in.

Stopping at a zebra crossing to let someone by, Gabe again wished he hadn't invited Hannah for coffee. Because instead of curbing his enthusiasm, Hannah's response had given him yet another reason to find her fascinating. As well as finding Hannah clever, funny and stubborn, it seemed Gabe could add *a walking contradiction* to his list.

He pictured Hannah's reaction. On the one hand, her eyes said she liked the idea of socialising with him. On the other, the words coming out of her mouth made it clear she didn't. Gabe frowned. It was as if Hannah wasn't sure what she wanted. He scoffed, forced to admit she wasn't the only one.

Negotiating a corner, Gabe told himself the fact that she'd turned him down was for the best. After all, he had enough friends already and he most certainly wasn't in the market for anything romantic. Proposing he and Hannah go for coffee might feel like a massive step, but in reality, it wasn't a big deal. Gabe let out a laugh. "So what if she said no?" Anyone would think he'd asked for Hannah's hand in marriage. Not to simply join him for a hot beverage, in a public place, something grown-ass adults did whether they were quixotically involved or not.

An image of the little white envelope popped into his head, but he didn't have the mental space to think about that too, so he pushed it away.

Gabe's pedalling slowed and bewildered, he recalled how Hannah hadn't just mentioned a flower delivery, she seemed to think it had come from him. He supposed it no wonder she'd read more into his coffee suggestion than was intended, although Gabe had to admit he hadn't exactly helped in that regard. Frustrated by his own stupidity, he reproached himself for not putting her straight on the matter.

Turning onto his road, the mystery flowers continued to play on Gabe's mind as he headed to the back of his house. There had to be a reason Hannah would think they were a gift from him. His eyes narrowed as an explanation began to show itself. "No. You wouldn't," he said.

Dismounting his bike, he wheeled it into the rear garden and after storing it in the shed, made his way into the kitchen. Taking the seat opposite, he stared at his dad, who read a newspaper at the table.

While most of the population kept themselves up to date with events via their phones, Roger preferred the old-fashioned approach. He could spend hours sitting there with his paper, reading every printed word. Roger even did the crossword; exercise for the brain as he called it. "Everything okay?" he asked, letting his newspaper drop.

"Not really."

Roger straightened up in his seat. "Why? What's happened now?"

Gabe raised his eyebrows. "I was hoping you could tell me."

"Animal, vegetable, or mineral?" Roger asked. "You're going to have to be a little more specific."

"Let's just say I saw Hannah earlier."

Roger picked his paper back up, raising it to the point that Gabe could no longer see his face. "I don't see what that has to do with me," he said from behind the page.

Gabe knew his dad was only pretending to read. That he was using the newspaper to hide behind. Gabe folded his arms and continuing to stare in his dad's direction, was happy to wait all day for Roger to give in if that's what it took.

At last, the paper fell for a second time. "I'm sorry, son," Roger said. "But I haven't seen you show an ounce of interest in anyone since... well, you know. Then this Hannah arrives on the scene and suddenly you're all gaga."

"Excuse me?"

"You know. Sitting there in some happy trance. The woman's clearly got under your skin, so I thought why not give things a little nudge. It's not like you were going to."

"But you've got no right to interfere like that, Dad. It's down to me to decide who I do and don't get involved with, not you."

Roger scoffed. "It was only a bunch of flowers. I didn't declare your undying love, Gabe."

Gabe thanked goodness for small mercies.

"I simply put your name and telephone number on one of those little card thingies, crossed my fingers and left it to the gods."

"My telephone number?" Gabe closed his eyes for a second. His insides felt like they were shrinking with his dad's every word. He thought it no wonder Hannah had turned him down for coffee. In not giving him a call, she'd already sent a clear message telling Gabe she wasn't interested. "Dad, how could you embarrass me like that?"

"Since when did sending a beautiful woman flowers become embarrassing?"

"The second she thanked me for something I knew nothing about."

"You didn't tell her that, did you?"

"For some unknown reason, no, I didn't."

"Then what's your problem?"

No way was Gabe telling his dad about the coffee invite. Instead of seeing it for what it was; a second rejection from Hannah, Roger would take it as positive proof his son was finally ready to move on. From that point forward, any woman who as much as stood in Gabe's eyeline wouldn't be safe from Roger's cupidesque efforts. Gabe shuddered. It would be like unleashing a matchmaking monster.

Gabe's phone bleeped indicating a text had landed. He tried to appear calm, but his heart leapt at the small chance it could be from Hannah. He looked to his dad who appeared to suddenly hold his breath in anticipation too. Pulling out his mobile and seeing the name on the screen, Gabe immediately felt deflated. "It's from Slim," he said, opening it up to read.

As Roger, at last, exhaled, his disappointment was obvious.

"He's asking if I fancy a drink tonight," Gabe said. He sighed. His friend being another one who thought he knew better.

CHAPTER 21

"*H*ow do I look?" Hannah asked, as she entered the lounge.

Halfway along a row, Aunt Dorothy stopped knitting to glance Hannah's way. She smiled. "Beautiful."

Hannah stared down at the white shirt and turned-up jeans that she'd teamed with a pair of red ballet pumps. Her hair was styled into a loose wispy chignon, and she wore the slightest of make-up. "I wouldn't go that far," she said. "But I'll do." Hannah paused in her thinking. "Are you sure you don't want to come?" She hated the thought of Dorothy sat home alone for the evening. "Mel and Liv would love to meet you. And you never know, you might have fun."

"Perfectly sure," Dorothy replied. "A night in front of the telly suits me fine."

"Well, I won't be late back," Hannah said, reluctantly picking up her handbag. "And I've got my phone. My number's written on a piece of paper next to the kettle should you need it. As is Mel and Liv's, just in case."

Dorothy got back to her knitting. "Take as long as you like."

With no choice but to leave her to it, Hannah headed out to

her car and climbed in. Starting up the engine, she couldn't remember the last time she'd eaten out. She often ordered in takeaway for herself and the kids, but to sit in an actual restaurant with proper waiters was a bit of a treat. Another reason to feel guilty, Hannah realised. Dorothy had spent hours that week slaving away in the kitchen and Hannah had a freezer full of freshly cooked meals to prove it.

Telling herself she'd make it up to Dorothy, Hannah put the car into gear and set off down the street. After signing up for the sponsored run, withdrawing and then signing up again, Liv had insisted on organising an *asap*, as she put it, *group meeting*; a meeting that, thanks to Hannah's stop/start commitment, she couldn't exactly get out of.

Driving along, Hannah's mind drifted back to her childhood visits to Norfolk. While Hannah's mum and dad had hit the tourist trail, Aunt Dorothy and Uncle Denis were happy to spend hours on the beach babysitting her. The three of them would build the hugest most-detailed sandcastles, complete with winding moats that they tried and failed to fill with sea water because it kept soaking away. Back then, Dorothy was jovial and outgoing. She had a zest for life. Uncle Denis's death had left her a shadow of the woman Hannah once knew. Emotionally and going off her weight loss, physically too.

Fast forwarding to present times, Hannah frowned as she recalled what her mum had said about giving Dorothy a fig biscuit and a mug of tea. An awful suggestion considering the numerous warm welcomes Dorothy had provided Hannah's family with over the years. Although she supposed in her mum's defence, Janice was a bit frazzled thanks to her extension woes. Hannah scoffed. What was her own excuse?

Dorothy's chat with Uncle Denis played through Hannah's mind. There was no denying her aunt's loneliness.

When it came to the death of a loved one, Hannah had always appreciated there was a grieving process and that no one person grieved the same. She understood that the person left behind might have to take responsibility for things they'd never had to deal with before: paying bills, DIY, housework, she supposed the list went on.

However, what Hannah had never considered, was the unlearning that Dorothy had talked about. Simple everyday things, like a shopping list that had become so second nature it didn't need writing down, suddenly having to be deconstructed and put back together again.

From what she'd said, Dorothy had had to go through all of it, the grief, the responsibility, and the unlearning all on her own.

Picturing her aunt sat staring at the television, Hannah took a deep breath. She slowed the car at a safe place, brought it to a standstill and switched off the engine. She pulled out her phone and dialled Liv's number. "About tonight," Hannah said when her friend answered.

CHAPTER 22

*H*aving turned her car round and gone home, Hannah smiled as she let herself back into the house.

"That was quick." Aunt Dorothy looked up as Hannah reappeared in the lounge. "Did you forget something?"

"Nope." Hannah slung her handbag down on the sofa. "If it's all right with you, we're holding the meeting here."

"But why?"

The last thing Hannah wanted was Dorothy thinking she pitied her and forced to think on her feet, Hannah blurted out the first excuse that popped into her head. "Apparently, our table was double booked."

Dorothy looked affronted. "But why cancel your party and not the other?" She put down her knitting and rose to her feet.

"Where are you going?" Having never seen her move so quickly, a part of Hannah thought her aunt was about to grab her jacket and head to the restaurant to demand an explanation.

Dorothy paused in the doorway. "To get dinner ready, of course. I bet none of you have eaten since lunch."

"But we can order takeout," Hannah called after her.

"Not on my watch, you can't," Dorothy said, marching down the hall to the kitchen.

Hannah giggled and shaking her head at her aunt's haste, followed her. "Need any help?"

"I can manage."

"At least let me lay the table."

"You'll do no such thing."

It wasn't long before the aroma of Dorothy's cooking once again filled the room and a knock at the door signalled Mel and Liv's arrival. "Sounds like they're here," Hannah said, heading down the hall to let them in.

"Thanks for this." Hannah kept her voice low so Dorothy wouldn't hear. "I've told her there was a table mix-up."

"Never mind that," Liv said. "What's on the menu? I can't tell you how hungry I am."

Hannah let out a laugh.

"I've had to listen to this non-stop for the last half an hour." Mel reached into her rucksack and pulled out a bottle of wine. "Mine's a large one."

"I'm sorry, but we've known each other too long for politeness," Liv said. "My stomach feels like my throat's been cut."

"Come on through and I'll introduce you to my aunt." Hannah led the way to the kitchen. "Aunt Dorothy, this is Mel and Liv."

Dorothy wiped her hands on a tea towel. "Pleased to meet you both." She immediately indicated they take a seat at the table. "Dinner's almost ready."

While Mel and Liv sat down Hannah dug out a corkscrew and opened the wine.

"Gorgeous flowers." Liv nodded to the profusion of pink blooms on the dresser.

"They're from Hannah's new man friend," Dorothy replied with a nod of her head. She gave Liv a pointed look. "A very handsome man friend, I might add."

Hannah recalled Gabe's obsidian eyes, thick dark hair and muscular frame. "I wouldn't go that far."

Her friends looked at her, their expressions a mix of curiosity and amazement.

"Why are we only just hearing about this?" Mel asked.

"Because it's nothing like what you're all thinking," Hannah replied.

"I think we'll be the judge of that," Liz said. "Come on. We want all the details."

Pouring everyone a glass of wine, Hannah sat down and relayed the events leading to Gabe escorting her home, making it clear she had no interest in him throughout.

"But to then send flowers," Mel said, once Hannah had finished.

"Exactly," Liv said. "The man's definitely into you."

"That's what I thought," Dorothy said.

Hannah took in everyone's eagerness. "This is exactly why I didn't say anything. I knew you'd see things that just aren't there."

Mel swooned, immediately proving Hannah's point. "Talk about a knight in shining armour."

Hannah scoffed. "Damage limitation more like. He was probably worried I'd sue."

"Where's your sense of romance?" Mel asked, crestfallen.

"I haven't got one."

"I hope he gave you his number," Liv said.

Knowing he had, Hannah suddenly felt a tad warm. "You're as bad as Aunt Dorothy," she said, not wanting to blatantly lie for a second time.

Dorothy placed a ceramic dish in the centre of the table. "Help yourselves." Setting down a ladle, she took a seat herself. "Anyone would think no one noticed the little wink he gave you before he left."

"He didn't," Mel said.

Dorothy nodded. "He certainly did."

Talk about her aunt being a troublemaker. Recalling the moment, Hannah felt her cheeks redden. "That doesn't mean anything."

"Then why are you blushing?" Mel asked, with a grin.

"The lady doth protest too much," Liv said.

"You forgot to mention the coffee invite you turned down," Dorothy said.

Hannah willed Dorothy to stop encouraging her friends, but their excitement grew regardless.

"What coffee invite?" Mel said.

"Was this before or after the flowers?" Liv asked.

"Why did you turn it down?" they both said.

The latter was a question Hannah continued to ask herself. "Never mind that, I thought you were both hungry," she said, avoiding having to answer. "It's time to eat."

Good manners meant allowing her guests to help themselves first. However, watching Liv spoon ladle after ladle onto her plate, Hannah had to wonder if there'd be enough left for the rest of them.

Evidently feeling the weight of Hannah's stare, Liv stopped what she was doing. "What?" she asked.

Hannah indicated her friend hand over the utensil.

Finally, everyone was served and Hannah looked down at the beef casserole adorning her plate. Packed with meat, onions, carrots and celery, which were topped with creamy sweet potato mash, like Liv, she was starving. As she dived straight in, Hannah's tastebuds immediately hit on the garlic and parsley. She closed her eyes, savouring the flavours. "Why does food always taste better when someone else cooks it?"

"When you're done here can you come and stay with me, Aunt Dorothy," Mel said. "This is delicious."

Too busy eating to say anything, Liv gave an emphatic nod.

"Speaking of white knights, any news on Russel?" Hannah asked.

Mel wrinkled up her nose and shook her head. "I've been thinking about what you said though. About me being the one to move things on. And I agree. I'm a modern woman, in a modern world and all that." She seemed to be trying to convince herself as much as she was everyone else.

"Mel met Russel online," Hannah said to Dorothy.

"And you've yet to get together in person?" Dorothy appeared impressed. "How thrilling."

"I'm planning on suggesting a date," Mel replied. "I just haven't yet plucked up the courage."

Hannah gave her arm a reassuring rub. "You will when you're ready."

"As will you," Dorothy said to Hannah, with a cheeky smile.

Hannah turned her attention to Liv. "Liv, here, is dating a vegan."

Liv paused in her eating. A chunk of beef sat on the spoon that was halfway to her mouth. "I'm doing a bit more than that," she said, letting out a naughty laugh. She came over all dreamy. "Quentin and I have just spent the most passionate couple of days together." She sighed at the memory, before bringing herself back into the room. "Why do you think I'm so hungry?"

"Liv!" Hannah and Mel chorused, while Dorothy suddenly guffawed. Talking about sex at the dinner table was bad enough, to discuss it in front of Dorothy was something else.

"I didn't mean that," Liv said. "I was talking about the lack of proper food on offer. I'm a farmer's daughter, remember." She proceeded to clear her plate of every scrap.

Food eaten, Hannah helped Dorothy clear the table, while Liv reached for her bag. "I suppose we should get down to business," she said. "That is why we're here, after all." She pulled out two A4 envelopes with a flourish. Pleased, she set one down on the table for Hannah and handed the other to Mel. "Your sponsorship forms."

"Ooh, exciting," Mel said, glancing inside.

"Although I'm wondering if it might be easier if we all just shared the one," Liv said. "What do all you think?"

"I agree," Hannah said. "As long as I don't have to collect it all."

Liv reached into her bag and grabbed a pen. "Don't worry. I'm happy to do that."

"Beth and Archie have already pledged. Oh, and Carl, too," Hannah said.

Liv made a note.

"But that's as far as I've got up to now."

"I'll sponsor you all too," Dorothy said.

"Work have said they're happy to pledge," Mel said. "And before I forget, I too come bearing gifts." Grabbing her rucksack, she delved inside. Producing a bright pink T-shirt, she held it up for everyone to see. "What do you think?"

Hannah and Dorothy snickered at the slogan emblazoned across the back.

"I thought they said rum," Hannah read out loud. She looked from one friend to the other. "Which one of you came up with that?"

"Neither of us," Mel replied. "I saw them on Etsy and couldn't resist. There's one for each of us." She looked to Dorothy. "I have extra if you'd like one too?"

"Oh, I'm not sure I'm up to running," Dorothy replied. "But thank you for asking."

"Don't think you're getting out of it altogether," Liv said. "We need you on the team."

Hannah smiled at her friends, grateful they'd taken her worries about Dorothy on board.

Dorothy looked to Hannah, her expression a mix of uncertainty and hope.

Hannah knew what she was thinking. Despite Hannah saying she could stay as long as she liked, Dorothy didn't really know if she'd be welcome for such an extended visit. Especially with

Hannah's foot a lot better. "You weren't planning on running back to Norfolk just yet, were you?"

"Hannah's already backed out of this race once," Liv continued. "And now she's back in, we need someone to make sure she stays in."

"Maybe we could get you a whistle and a stopwatch," Mel said. "That way you can keep us *all* on target."

"Would I get a title?" Dorothy asked. "Like Mrs Motivator?"

Hannah envisaged the three of them running along a racetrack, with her aunt pedalling a bike beside. Screaming at them to get a move on, Dorothy had a timer hanging around her neck and a loudhailer to her lips.

"We can do better than that. You'd be the team leader," Liv said.

Dorothy looked from Hannah to the others, as if not sure what to say. Her eyes glistened in a mix of tears and joy. "I'd love that. If Hannah's sure she doesn't mind?"

"Of course I don't mind. I think it's a great idea." Hannah gave her aunt a pretend frown. "Although you're going to have to stop feeding me food like this. It's salads from here on in."

Mel let out a laugh. "You don't have to eat rabbit food. I've told you. When it comes to running, it's all in the breathing."

"That's easy for you to say. You're an Olympic champion."

"Are you?" Dorothy asked.

Mel shook her head. "Hardly."

"Either way, I couldn't breathe full stop the day Gabe hit me. I'm convinced that's why I got run over. The lack of oxygen affected my eyesight."

"If you're worried about your fitness," Liv said, "I'm sure Quentin's mentioned one of his friends is a personal trainer. I'll see if he can arrange a session for you if you like?"

"I don't know about that." Hannah looked down at her wholesome figure. "I'm not sure I want some health freak judging my lifestyle choices."

"Think of the team," Dorothy said, her accompanying sternness telling Hannah she already took her new role seriously.

"We're not suggesting a lifetime commitment," Liv said. "The race is only a couple of weeks away. After that, you can kiss the man's services goodbye."

Hannah looked from Liv to Mel to Dorothy. Going off their expressions it didn't seem she had much choice. "Okay," she said, at last relenting. "I'll give it a go."

"Excellent." Liv clapped her hands together in excitement. "Wouldn't it be funny if you ended up with two buff men sending you flowers."

"No," Hannah replied, deadpan. "It would not."

CHAPTER 23

*B*ack in her jogging pants and new trainers, Hannah made her way downstairs. She felt anxious. She'd never had a personal trainer before and despite not knowing what to expect, it already felt way outside her comfort zone. Yet again, she found herself wondering why she'd agreed to do the run in the first place.

Entering the kitchen, she chuckled at the sight of Aunt Dorothy, who wore her pink running team T-shirt as she busied herself chopping a variety of fruit and placing it all in a cereal bowl.

"Breakfast is served," she said, placing her spoils on the table next to a waiting glass of orange juice.

Hannah sat down. Looking at the segments of banana, apple, satsuma, and melon, she couldn't help but smile. From their team meeting onwards, Dorothy had thrown herself into her role. "You don't have to do this," Hannah said. "I'm sure being my chief cook and however the saying goes..." It was early. Hannah's brain hadn't yet kicked into gear. Plus, she was about to embarrass herself in front of a fitness fanatic. "Isn't in your job description."

"Speaking of which…" Dorothy grabbed Hannah's water bottle from the counter and placed it in front of her. "Voila!"

Looking at it, Hannah wondered how she was going to manage when the time came for her aunt to head home to Norfolk. Hannah had hardly had to lift a finger in the kitchen following Dorothy's arrival and getting back into the swing of doing everything again was going to be hard. Having someone around to help had made Hannah realise just how little Beth and Archie did around the house.

"If a job's worth doing," Dorothy said.

Dorothy might have been talking about her job on the team, but it was a sentiment Hannah often used in her role as a mother. Sometimes she'd end the phrase with *it's worth doing well* and at others she ended it with *then do it yourself*. She sighed. More often it was the latter.

Picking up her fork, Hannah had more urgent matters to think about and as she dug into a segment of apple and stuffed it in her mouth, she turned her thoughts to the fitness guru about to knock on her door. Hoping she wasn't about to embarrass herself too much, she felt Dorothy watching her as she chewed.

"Is everything okay?" Dorothy asked.

"I'm nervous about this personal trainer thing. Let's face it, I'm not exactly the sportiest of people. I never have been."

"You'll be fine."

Hannah wished she had her aunt's confidence. "It might be years since I was at school, but you're talking to the girl who no one wanted on their team." She laughed. "That kind of leaves a mark."

Back in Hannah's day, nerd chic didn't exist. Being academic meant nothing on or off the netball court. So if, like her, being bookish was all you had going for you, you definitely weren't considered one of the cool kids. Week after week in PE, when it came to choosing teams, Hannah had to listen to team captains call out everyone else's name but hers. She could still see their disdain when she was the only person left and had to join their ranks regardless. Hannah sighed. "I just hope this chap Liv's organised has more understanding."

"You're worrying over nothing," Dorothy said. "I'm sure Liv wouldn't set you up with a drill sergeant." She picked up her mug of tea and joined Hannah at the table. "You always were more brains than brawn. As a child, you'd read anything and everything you could get your hands on. And the constant questions... Sometimes my head hurt, you asked so many. Politics, literature, art, no matter the subject you queried something. It was like you had a sponge in your head soaking up as much information as it could get. Denis and I had visions of you becoming prime minister one day."

"And look at me now. Things couldn't be more different." Hannah smiled, wistful. "I had such big plans when I was younger. Maybe not to run a country, but I wanted to pass my course..."

"Which you did."

"Then I wanted to start my own interior design company."

Dorothy glanced around. "That explains the beautiful house."

"It's surprising what you can do on a budget, which is why I was going to specialise in it. Helping people create beautiful homes without having to spend a fortune. Of course, that's nothing new today. Everyone seems to be doing it. You only have to scroll through Instagram reels and Pinterest to see that. But I've always been a bargain hunter. Since well before it was fashionable."

"So what stopped you?"

"Soon after finishing uni I fell pregnant. When I found out we were having twins, I didn't have much choice but to put my ideas on hold. Looking after two babies at the same time was going to be challenging enough. Plus, childcare for one cost a fortune, for two it was extortionate."

"Still, having to give up your plans must have been hard."

"Carl was training to be a lawyer at the time, so in the long run it made sense for him to be the breadwinner. That's when I decided I'd put my business career to good use and treat being a full-time mum like I would any other career. I'd be the best, most efficient mum on the planet." Hannah picked up her glass of orange and took a drink. "Once the kids were in school and I could think about my design business again, Carl decided to up and leave." She scoffed. "He felt we didn't have anything in common anymore. Which meant I had to take any job I could get to bring some money in. I've worked at the call centre ever since."

"It's not too late though. You're still young. Why not start your business now?"

"Like I said, designing on a budget is trendy these days. What I had to offer back then, people are now doing of their own accord."

"Then come up with another idea," Dorothy suggested. "Beth and Archie are of an age where they can fend for themselves."

Not for the first time, Hannah recalled her mum's comment about the kids going off to university in the not-too-distant future. As well as a new chapter in their lives, she supposed it could be a new one in hers too. It would certainly give her a purpose once they'd gone. "Maybe I will."

"In the meantime, you know what's needed around here?" Dorothy said. "A bit of fun."

Hannah laughed. "What do you suggest?"

"I haven't a clue. But I'm sure between us we'll think of something." Suddenly animated, Dorothy's eyes lit up. "We could include Mel and Liv. Make it a group activity. Like a team bonding exercise."

"Why not," Hannah said. Enjoying her enthusiasm, it was great to see a glimpse of the Aunt Dorothy of old. "Count me in."

Hannah cocked her head at the sound of the doorbell. "That's if I don't twist another ankle in the interim." Imagining she was about to get a beasting, her heart raced as she got up from her seat and headed down the hall. Grabbing one of Archie's baseball caps off the coat stand, she put it on. If things got too embarrassing, at least wearing that she could pull the peak down to disguise her identity.

Pausing, Hannah took a deep breath to calm herself before answering. Fixing a friendly face in readiness, she flung the door open. Her expression froze. "Gabe," she said, without moving her lips.

He stood there looking as handsome as ever, this time in a pair of running shorts and a tight-fitting T-shirt. "Hannah," he replied.

Up until the previous week, she'd never clapped eyes on Gabe. But from the second she had, she couldn't seem to get rid of him. She waited for Gabe to tell her what he wanted, but he seemed to be expecting her to speak first. "Can I help you?" she asked at last.

Her question appeared to throw him. "I thought I was here to help you."

"To do what?" Hannah replied, equally confused.

"With your training session."

She stared at Gabe. "You mean you're…?"

"Your PT instructor?" He clearly found the situation funny. "I am, indeed. Slim asked if I'd step in."

"Who's Slim?" Hannah had never heard of the man.

"I believe his new partner's a friend of yours. I think her name's Liv?"

"But Liv's boyfriend's name is…" Hannah fell silent as realisation dawned. "Oh, I get it. He's named after Slim, as in Fatboy."

Gabe's smile grew.

"Otherwise known as Norman Cook. Real name *Quentin* Leo Cook."

"I'm impressed."

"Small world," Hannah said. Although having already shown

herself up once in front of Gabe on the running front, she didn't relish the prospect of doing it again.

His delight continued. "Isn't it."

Hannah heard a titter from behind and she turned to see Aunt Dorothy. Watching them from the kitchen doorway, she wore a grin bigger than Gabe's.

"Nice to see you again," she said.

"You too," Gabe replied.

"Beautiful flowers, by the way."

Recalling the last time Dorothy had come face to face with Gabe, Hannah was surprised the woman could string a sentence together.

"I hope you'll stay for a cuppa after you're done," Dorothy said, her tone mischievous.

Narrowing her eyes, Hannah knew there'd be a motive behind Dorothy's invitation, and Hannah hazarded a guess it related to their team conversation about her love life, or lack of, the other evening. However, Dorothy, Mel and Liv were in for a surprise if they thought they could matchmake. Since Beth and Archie had left for France, Hannah's life felt emotionally complicated enough. "He can't," Hannah said.

"Why not?" Dorothy asked, bemused.

"Because Gabe and I now have a professional relationship. Tea would create a conflict of interest or a confidentiality issue." She turned to him. "Isn't that right?"

Gabe let out a laugh. "I'd agree if I was a doctor or a priest. But I'm not here to take your temperature *or* hear your confession." He looked to Dorothy. "Thank you. That would be lovely."

While Hannah stood there trying to come up with another excuse, Gabe rubbed his hands together.

"Now we've got that cleared up," he said. "Shall we get started?"

CHAPTER 24

Telling Aunt Dorothy she'd see her soon, Hannah stepped outside and closed the door behind her. She felt self-conscious standing next to Gabe. He wasn't only handsome, he was fitness personified. In comparison, with all her lumps and bumps, she looked like a sack of potatoes.

"It's best practice to start with a few stretches," Gabe said.

Getting straight into their session, Hannah had thought he'd ease her in with a bit of chit-chat. Gabe had to know she was nervous, and a bit of conversation, however insignificant the subject, might have helped put Hannah at ease.

"It's important to warm up the muscles to prevent unnecessary injuries."

"Okay," Hannah said, surprised to find she'd learned something already. Thinking back, the stitch she'd experienced during her last attempt at running had clearly been caused by a lack of due diligence on the preparation front.

Gabe raised his arms above his head, pulling first on one elbow and then on the other. Hannah couldn't help but admire his physique. Even his muscles appeared to have muscles.

Watching him, she felt hot and bothered, something she couldn't blame on exercise because she hadn't started yet.

"This is a triceps stretch," he said, indicating Hannah follow his lead.

Glancing round at the neighbouring houses to make sure the curtain twitchers weren't nosing, Hannah tugged on the bottom of her T-shirt before doing as she was told. Hoping she didn't look too stupid, she told herself it was needs must.

After a few moments, Gabe dropped his arms ready to move on to the next part of their workout. Clasping his hands together, he bent his right knee for balance, while throwing his left leg out to the side. "We call this a side lunge."

Again, Hannah copied his actions, albeit with less poise.

Gabe talked her through a couple more exercises, before insisting they shake themselves out to loosen up. Thanking goodness she was wearing a sports bra, humiliation threatened to overwhelm Hannah as she jiggled her body from head to toe.

At last, it seemed they were good to go.

Already sweating, Hannah steeled herself. Embarrassing warm-ups were one thing. Jogging next to a Greek god was something else.

"Don't worry," Gabe said, as if reading her mind. "We won't be doing any running today."

"Really?" Hannah immediately relaxed, relieved to hear it.

"One, I need to make sure your ankle's okay after last week's fall. I know you've been testing it out, but it would be good for me to see it for myself."

"Fair enough."

"And two, walking enables me to assess your overall fitness so I can come up with an effective training regime."

Listening to him, Gabe sounded quite the professional. Something Hannah had to admit she thought sexy. "Sounds good to me," she said. Strolling along with a handsome man at her side, what was there not to like.

"When it comes to your breathing, remember it's in through your nose and out through your mouth." He took a deep nasal breath and exhaled as described.

Watching him repeat the action, Hannah found the rise and fall of his chest mesmerising.

"Your turn," he said.

Copying his actions, Hannah too breathed in and out.

"Excellent," Gabe said, leaving Hannah surprisingly chuffed at the compliment.

As they set off down the street, it seemed Hannah's happiness was short-lived. A stroll was clearly the last thing on Gabe's mind. Hannah struggled to keep up and before they'd even got to the end of the terrace she felt short of breath. "Do we have to go this fast?" She seemed to be walking faster than she could run.

Gabe stopped to look at Hannah. "We're not taking a Saturday morning walkabout."

Hannah felt tears threatening her eyes. It was as if the years had faded away and Hannah was back in school faced with a less-than-understanding team captain. She stared back at Gabe, wondering what had happened to the caring man she'd previously met. The Gabe who'd sat down next to her on the pavement and listened to her snivelling. The Gabe who'd sent her a cocktail of pink flowers, invited her for coffee, and had just agreed to join Dorothy for a cup of tea. Equally as important, the Gabe who only moments before had admired her breathing. "I know that," Hannah said. "But your legs are longer than mine. I'm taking two steps to your one."

Gabe relaxed his stance. "Look, no one expects you to win this race you've signed up to. But it would be good if you could at least finish it, don't you think?"

What Hannah wanted was to go home.

A picture of Beth and Archie's pride during their last video call popped into Hannah's head and knowing she didn't want to disappoint them, she realised she'd no choice but to pull herself together. She nodded in answer to Gabe's question.

"Well then. Let's go," he said, setting off again.

"Let's go," Hannah mimicked behind his back.

Picking up her pace to try to catch up with him, it seemed Dorothy had been wrong in her assertion about Liv. As it turned out, her friend would, indeed, set Hannah up with a drill sergeant.

Hannah frowned. She was convinced at any moment Gabe would start shouting *Left! Left! Left, right, Left!*

CHAPTER 25

The sound of chatter filtered up from the kitchen. Hannah frowned, picturing Aunt Dorothy and Gabe laughing and joking over their cups of tea. Gabe had evidently switched back to his original personality and Dorothy was, no doubt, further beguiled.

Hannah strained to hear what they were saying but couldn't decipher a word. "You might be able to fool her," she said of Gabe. "But you can't fool me." Hannah had seen first-hand what lay underneath all that Greek god deliciousness. As far as she was concerned, the man was a monster.

She continued to scowl as she got dressed. Going off the noise, the two of them clearly weren't missing her. Still, having spent long enough in the shower, Hannah knew she couldn't loiter in the bathroom forever. She winced as she put on her slippers thanks to the blisters on her heels, and dragging her feet as she went, she made her way downstairs to join them.

Hannah stopped in the doorway, surprised to see Dorothy and Gabe weren't alone.

"Feeling better?" Dorothy asked, spotting Hannah's arrival.

"What's going on?" Hannah's eyes went from her aunt, to Mel, to Liv, and then Gabe, who wore bright pink. "And why is he wearing one of our T-shirts?"

"We're having a meeting," Dorothy said. "To organise the team bonding session we talked about earlier. I rang Mel and Liv on the numbers you left me the other evening. And Gabe was already here, of course."

"I still can't believe your Gabe and my Quentin are friends," Liv said, interrupting.

Hannah couldn't believe Liv was calling him *her* Gabe. She cringed, not daring to look at the man to see what he thought.

Dorothy carried on. "We were waiting for you before making a final decision."

"And I was just telling everyone about my upcoming date with Russel," Mel said. "I know it's only online. But finally. Oh, and I have a picture. Would you like to see it?" She pulled out her phone and excitedly passed it to Hannah. "Isn't he handsome."

Hannah took in Russel's reddish blond hair and black-framed glasses. With a square jaw and great cheekbones, Hannah could see why Mel considered him good looking. However, with not even a hint of a smile, Russel's intense blue eyes stared straight into the camera lens. His expression was so serious, in fact, Hannah couldn't tell if he was exceedingly nervous about having his picture taken or planning a murder. "He looks lovely," she said, passing the phone along so everyone got the chance to see it.

"I can't believe I took your advice, Hannah. Who'd have thought it? Me, making the first proper move?" She clapped her hands together before suddenly falling quiet. She looked from Hannah to Gabe. "I take it this morning didn't go too well?"

"It could have been better," Gabe said.

Hannah flashed him her best dirty look.

"Although it could also have been worse," Gabe added, clearly opting for damage limitation.

"Never mind that," Liv said. "You'll both get over it."

Hannah wasn't so sure.

"Aunt Dorothy's come up with a great suggestion as to what we should do," Liv continued. "Although I must warn you, it's going to be tricky to organise."

"I'm sure between us we can find a way," Dorothy said. "This is not a team of quitters."

Gabe snickered and Hannah threw him another glower. If looks could kill, he'd have been on the floor.

Dorothy's delight faltered. "Is everything okay, Hannah? I thought you'd be pleased. You seemed keen this morning."

Hannah knew she was being childish, but she was still bitter about the beasting Gabe had given her. "Apart from the fact that *he* just tried to kill me and while I'm upstairs recovering, you're all socialising with a wannabe murderer, you mean?"

"Stop exaggerating," Dorothy said, not even attempting to hide her amusement.

It was all right for her. She wasn't the one who'd spent the morning being marched from street to street to street, all the while begging for mercy.

"I did tell you it's all in the breathing," Mel said, while Liv sucked in her lips clearly trying not to laugh.

"And I was only doing my job," Gabe said.

"Only doing your job? You saw the state of me." Hannah recalled the mess she was in when they'd landed back. With her hair stuck to her forehead and sweat dripping down her beetroot red face, she'd been on the verge of passing out. Be it through a lack of oxygen or overheating, neither would have been a good way to go. She didn't know how she'd found the energy to climb the stairs to the bathroom. "You still haven't told me why you're here."

Mel beamed. "He's here because he's part of the team."

Hannah looked to the rest of the group. "Since when?" She wondered if it was too late to veto his membership.

"Since ten minutes ago," Liv said. "As well as working with you, Gabe has kindly agreed to organise some group training sessions. At the sports centre in town. And for free considering we're running this race for charity."

Not intent on one victim, Gabe was obviously a serial killer. "Very civic," Hannah said.

Dorothy stood to give Hannah her chair. "Come and sit down. I'll make you a cuppa." She shook her head in continued hilarity as she proceeded to the kettle.

"Can I have some sympathy with that tea, please?" Hannah asked, taking a seat as instructed. "So, what's this bonding idea you've come up with?"

"Let's just say it involves Danny Parkes."

Hannah raised an eyebrow. "As in the singer?"

Dorothy swooned. "The one and only."

She wore the same expression Beth did whenever she heard his name.

"Aunt Dorothy thinks we should all go to his gig," Mel said. "And I have to say, I agree."

Gabe straightened up in his seat. "If it's okay with you lot, I think I'll pass."

Hannah could see why he wouldn't be up for the concert. He didn't match the Danny Parkes fan base. But after what Gabe had put her through that morning, Hannah immediately jumped on the chance to pay him back. She put on her best innocent face. "Like Aunt Dorothy said, Gabe. This *is* a team bonding activity. You're one of us now. I'm afraid you've no choice."

"Of course you don't have to come, Gabe," Liv said. "Ignore her." She turned to Hannah, amused. "What's got into you today?"

Hannah ignored the question. "Actually, I don't think any of us can go," she said instead. "We'll have to think of something else." Hannah recalled Beth's devastation when she learned Danny's concert had sold out in minutes. That was the only reason Beth had happily gone to the South of France. "There are no tickets available."

"Hence, its trickiness," Liv said. "Surely with a bit of ingenuity, we can sort something out."

"What kind of ingenuity?" Hannah asked. "We're not just talking about one or two people getting in. There are five of us."

"Whatever we do we need to go big," Liv said. "Because one of us isn't going to be around for much longer."

Hannah's eyes widened in horror. She looked from Liv to Dorothy and back again. "I hope you're referring to the fact that Aunt Dorothy lives in Norfolk."

Liv let out a laugh. "Why?"

"Because Aunt Dorothy might be in her seventies, but she's fit and healthy." Hannah turned to face her aunt. "You've got years left in you, haven't you?"

"I certainly hope so," Dorothy said, laughing.

"I'm not talking about Aunt Dorothy, Hannah," Liv explained. "I'm talking about me."

"What do you mean?" Hannah felt a sudden panic. "You're not sick, are you?"

"Of course not." Liv looked at Hannah aghast. "Whatever gave you that idea?"

Hannah's relief was palpable. "Your rubbish choice of words might have something to do with it."

Liv tilted her head. "I meant Mel's not the only one with relationship news." She took a deep breath. "I wasn't planning on saying anything just yet, but..." Liv paused, obviously for dramatic effect.

An engagement, moving in together, buying a dog... Hannah wished Liv would just tell them.

Liv's smiled. "Quentin's asked me to go to Africa with him."

"He's done what?" Hannah asked, hoping she'd misheard.

"And are you going to?" Mel asked.

"I'm thinking about it," Liv replied.

Hannah didn't know what to say. Liv and Quentin, Mel and Russel, Carl and Monica... She was pleased for them, of course. It was the fact that everyone was moving on in their lives while she remained static that unsettled her. Shocked, Hannah turned to Gabe. "Did you know about this?"

He shrugged; an action Hannah took to mean yes.

Hannah returned her attention to Liv. Out of all the relationship news her friend could have shared, Hannah didn't expect that.

CHAPTER 26

TWO WEEKS UNTIL RACE DAY

*R*aising her legs slightly, Hannah wiggled her heels to make sure the plasters covering them stayed securely in place. Satisfied they weren't going anywhere, the last thing she needed were yet more blisters. "I don't see why *I* can't drive us there," Hannah said, carefully putting on her socks and trainers. Another thing Hannah didn't need was to be stuck in a car with Gabe. She'd still not fully forgiven him for what he'd put her through during their one-to-one training session. Or for not giving her the heads up on Liv's potential trip to Africa.

"Maybe he wants to make sure you turn up," Dorothy said, her expression mischievous. "Perhaps he saw it as a chance for you both to get better acquainted? Flowers, coffee date. He probably thinks third time lucky."

"What are you talking about?" Hannah asked.

"It's obvious the man likes you."

Not to Hannah it wasn't. "Is that why he's trying to kill me?"

"For once, it would be nice for him to see the real you," Dorothy said.

"Ah, but that's where you're going wrong, Aunt Dorothy. Every time I've met Gabe, he's seen the real me. And if you think

121

he's interested after that, then you have to think the man's a sadist."

Dorothy shook her head. "You are funny."

Hannah eyed her aunt, suspicious. "You asked him for a lift, didn't you?"

"I might have done."

At least the woman was honest.

Dorothy added her knitting to the bag of provisions she'd put together. A flask of tea, bottles of water, oranges, crisps and a packet of biscuits; what Aunt Dorothy called essentials, Hannah called a picnic. "You didn't exactly embrace your last training session, Hannah."

Hannah sighed, forced to admit she had whinged more than usual during their one-to-one. Moreover, she hadn't exactly welcomed him onto the team afterwards. All things considered, if Aunt Dorothy was hoping to upgrade Hannah's reputation, she was on to a loser. "I suppose I was a bit of a baby."

Dorothy laughed. "A bit?"

"In my defence, you didn't see what he put me through. I'm telling you, as personality changes go, that man's worse than Jekyll and Hyde."

Dorothy laughed again, while a knock at the door indicated Gabe's arrival.

"It might help if you remember you're not entering the Olympics," Dorothy said. "Charity runs are meant to be fun. At least try to enjoy yourself."

"Easy for you to say."

Gabe was back behind the wheel by the time Dorothy and Hannah exited the house. Hannah indicated her aunt sit in the front seat and locking the door behind them, she climbed into the rear with Dorothy's provisions bag.

Dorothy and Gabe chatted amiably as they drove to the sports centre. She told him how much she was relishing her stay and he suggested a few local attractions that she might want to visit.

Gabe behaved nothing like the drill sergeant he'd been the last time Hannah saw him. Gabe was relaxed and showed interest when Dorothy talked knitting patterns and was patient when she went into great detail about her favourite soap opera's latest storyline.

Listening to the two of them, Hannah felt guilty for the things she'd said about Gabe. Maybe Dorothy was right. Maybe Hannah was taking the sponsored run too seriously. Maybe she took everything too seriously.

Gabe looked at Hannah through the rear-view mirror. "You're quiet back there."

Meeting his gaze, their eyes locked for a moment and Hannah had to blink herself free. "Just enjoying the ride."

"She's conserving her energy," Dorothy said, clearly hell-bent on showing Hannah in a good light.

While Gabe returned his attention to the road, Hannah stared out of the side window. Watching the world go by, she was determined to enjoy that evening like Dorothy had suggested.

At last, reaching their destination, Gabe pulled up at the entrance so Dorothy and Hannah could alight, before he drove off to find a proper parking space. "Leave that," he said as Hannah took hold of Dorothy's bag. "I'll bring it."

Seeing Mel and Liv already there to greet them, Hannah smiled. She looked forward to a quick catch up before Gabe reappeared and put them to work. Spotting they weren't alone, her expression froze and her stomach sank. "What's *she* doing here?"

CHAPTER 27

*H*annah frowned, as she watched Francesca stare at her own reflection in the sports centre panes of glass. The woman faffed with her hair, making sure her long brunette ponytail remained perfect. Anyone would think they were about to take part in a fashion show not a workout session.

"She overheard us talking about the race," Mel said, keeping her voice low. "And invited herself onto the team."

"We don't want her here either, but we couldn't exactly say no," Liv said. "Not when it's all for charity."

Hannah appreciated their dilemma. Refusing to let Francesca join the team would have contradicted the public-spirited nature of the event. Plus, in her bid to be the best at everything, Francesca was bound to raise a tonne of money.

Suddenly clocking Hannah's reflection in the glass, Francesca turned to face her. "Hannah. How lovely to see you."

Francesca oozed confidence in her black Lycra leggings and the tightest of vest tops. Teamed with brilliant white trainers, the whole ensemble was obviously brand new, and Hannah would have put money on her buying the lot especially for the occasion. Hannah fake smiled. "Good to see you too."

Francesca raised her eyebrows. "I hope you're ready to run for your life."

It was just like Francesca to issue a challenge, Hannah considered. The woman couldn't seem to help herself. When they got down to it, she'd probably inform everyone they weren't taking enough steps per minute the way she did calls per hour at work.

Francesca looked to Dorothy. "And you are?"

Dorothy beamed with pride. "The team captain."

Francesca appeared momentarily confused, as if not sure she'd heard correctly. Suddenly, her expression relaxed, and she let out a laugh. "Good one," she said, shaking her head as if Dorothy had been joking. Turning her back on Dorothy altogether, Francesca addressed Mel and Liv. "I'll meet you inside."

"Don't take it personally," Hannah said. "She's like that with most people."

Dorothy scoffed. "I learnt not to do that a long time ago."

"Ready, ladies?" Appearing with Dorothy's bag, Gabe held the door open so everyone could enter.

As soon as he was inside, the girl on reception glanced in Gabe's direction. Her face broke into a big grin as soon as she saw him. "Gabe. Great to see you." She nodded towards the stairs. "You know the way."

Never one to be outshone by a pretty girl, Francesca appeared at Gabe's side.

Hannah felt a pang of irritation thanks to all the eyelash fluttering in the place.

"I'm Francesca." She held her hand out for Gabe to shake. "You should know, I'm also this motley crew's team leader." She made a disdainful show of glancing at the rest of the group. "I know, I know, but someone's got to sort them out."

"Have you heard her?" Mel asked, offended.

Liv scoffed. "The cheek of the woman."

Hannah simply shook her head.

"Come on, everyone," Francesca instructed. She paused to let Gabe lead the way. Despite trying to appear in the know, she obviously didn't have a clue where she was going.

Entering a huge gymnasium, Gabe headed straight for a long wooden bench, reminiscent of the one Hannah was often forced to sit on during PE at school. Refusing to see it as bad omen, Hannah lined up next to it with everyone else.

Putting the provisions bag down, Gabe pulled out a whistle from his tracksuit bottoms pocket. "This is for you, Aunt Dorothy," he said, holding it out for her to take.

Delighted, Dorothy squealed. "Do I get to use it?" Hanging it around her neck, she gave it a blast before he could answer.

"So childish," Francesca said, not even trying to hide her disdain.

Still focused on Dorothy, Gabe smiled and indicated she take a seat on the bench. As Dorothy got out her knitting, Gabe turned his attention to the rest of the group. "Ready, everyone?"

Oh, Lordy. Immediately recognising his authoritative expression, Hannah knew what they were all in for. She let out a whimper.

Gabe began by going through all the exercises he'd covered during his one-to-one session with Hannah. He grimaced at the varying results. Watching everyone was clearly painful viewing.

Hannah was as atrocious on that occasion as she had been the first time around. Not that Mel and Liv helped. Snickering at Hannah's lack of co-ordination to properly concentrate on what they were doing, the three of them ended up behaving like naughty school children. Francesca was clearly the swot of the group. Much to Hannah's annoyance, she followed Gabe's every move to the centimetre.

Once they'd jiggled sufficiently to loosen up, Gabe began outlining how the training session would go. "Tonight might be all about quick walking, but we'll be incorporating a slow jog here and there. Remember, it's important to concentrate on your breathing throughout."

Mel leaned into Hannah. "Told you."

"In through the nose," Gabe continued. "Out through the mouth." He paused as if to let his instruction sink in. "Our team leader here…"

Francesca stepped forward, gloating at what she evidently thought was special attention. Only to step back when Gabe turned to Dorothy.

"… will signal when to start."

Hannah mumbled to herself. "That'll teach you," she said of Francesca.

"On the first blow of the whistle, you walk," Gabe continued. "When you hear the second, you jog. When you hear the third, you go back to walking. And so on." Gabe scanned the group. "Is that clear?"

Hannah nodded along with the rest of group.

Gabe signalled to Dorothy, who blew long and hard on her whistle.

Hannah and the others immediately set off on a walk around the gymnasium perimeter.

Unsurprisingly to Hannah, Francesca set the pace when she strode ahead. Francesca was always boasting about her exclusive gym membership and fantastic fitness level, but it wasn't long before Mel caught up with her. While the two of them jostled for position, Hannah and Liv brought up the rear, a placement Hannah was happy with.

Walking at a steadier rate than her forerunners, Hannah was cheered by how comfortable she felt. Her ankle-testing walks had obviously built up her stamina.

"Look at her go," Liv said, as Mel suddenly left Francesca for dust.

Elbows bent and hips swinging, Mel didn't seem to care that she looked like a penguin on speed.

"No wonder she still holds Saint Hilda's running record," Hannah said. Mel's competitiveness seemed to know no bounds.

"It's good of Gabe to do this, isn't it?" Liv asked.

"It is." Hannah glanced over at him, but quickly diverted her eyes when he suddenly returned her gaze.

"I'm still in shock that he's friends with Quentin. I mean, what are the odds of that? Did I tell you I'm going to a rally on Saturday?"

"No, you didn't," Hannah replied.

"It's to protest cotton capitalism."

Hannah frowned. "I think you mean climate change."

"Do I?"

"Cotton capitalism is something to do with the 1800s."

"Is it?"

"I'm sure I read somewhere it's linked to slavery."

"Well, whatever I mean, it's something Quentin feels strongly about. It's one of the reasons he works in non-profit. Apparently, carbon emissions from cotton production amount to millions and millions of metric tonnes a year. And did you know, well over 2000 litres of water are needed to produce a single cotton T-shirt?"

"Wow," Hannah said. "That's terrible."

As Liv continued to witter, Hannah began to feel the effects of her walking. She struggled to breathe and talk at the same time and had to respond to Liv with one-word answers. *In through the nose and out through the mouth* became her internal mantra as she concentrated on putting one foot in front of the other.

"I've come up with a great idea for our team bonding session. I was thinking we could all go for a meal. Not just us though, it would be great to invite Quentin and Russel."

By then Hannah struggled to speak completely.

"It would be like a triple date," Liv said, excited.

Hannah wanted to stop and tell her friend that, no, it would not be like that at all, but she knew if she did, she wouldn't get going again.

The shrill of Dorothy's whistle suddenly pierced the room and Hannah grimaced.

"Come on, Hannah. Start running," Gabe called out. "You too, Liv. You heard the whistle." He turned his attention to Mel and Francesca who were quicker off the mark. "Great job, you two."

Hannah silently cursed the man as she broke into a jog. Only to jump when Mel flew passed her shoulder, quickly followed by Francesca. Hannah couldn't believe she and Liv had been lapped, something she knew Francesca would never let them live down.

Embarrassed, Hannah tried to pick up pace, only to suddenly feel a pain shoot up the inner side of her tibia. Wondering why she was putting herself through hell, shin splints were all Hannah needed.

Wishing she was anywhere but there, her making it through the session was going to take a miracle.

CHAPTER 28

*H*annah sat on the back seat of Gabe's car, listening to Aunt Dorothy chat to Gabe about how wonderful the training session had been. Just like earlier, he seemed genuinely interested in her thoughts and Hannah was pleased to hear that her aunt had enjoyed herself. The following day's pain she was, no doubt, going to experience was worth it for that alone.

"Hark at me wittering on," Dorothy said. "I haven't let you get a word in, Gabe. Please, tell me something about you."

"There isn't much to tell," Gabe replied. "My life's pretty boring to be honest."

"I can't believe that." Dorothy paused as if trying to conjure up the right words. "Is there a Mrs Gabe on the scene at all?"

Hannah's ears pricked and her eyes widened. Wondering what her aunt was playing at, she couldn't believe the direction in which Dorothy had steered their conversation. Having insisted Gabe liked Hannah from the start, the woman was evidently on a fishing expedition. Even worse, Dorothy couldn't have been less subtle if she tried. Hannah cringed and sliding down in her seat, willed her aunt to please shut up.

Gabe looked at Hannah through his rear-view mirror. Just like her, he clearly knew what Dorothy was up to. "No." He smiled and gave Hannah a wink. "There's no Mrs Gabe."

Hannah blushed, and ignoring the little flutter in her chest, indignantly insisted his relationship status had nothing to do with her.

"Oh, that is good," Dorothy said, adding to Hannah's discomfort.

As Gabe drove onto Hannah's street, Hannah looked forward to a soak in the bath. One, so she could wash away her embarrassment. And two, so she could ease her pain. Despite the majority of the group's claim that the night's training session was a success, for Hannah it felt anything but. She was knackered, her feet hurt, and because she'd failed to master the correct breathing technique, so did her throat.

Hannah had known from the start she'd have to work to bring her fitness level up. However, she hadn't realised just how out of shape she'd become. As team members went, it was clear Hannah was the weakest link.

"I hope you're coming in for a cup of tea?" Dorothy asked Gabe, as he pulled up outside the house. "That's okay with you, isn't it, Hannah?"

Despite wanting to, Hannah didn't have the energy to protest. "That's fine with me." After all, she'd be soothing her muscles in the bath anyway. A little voice wondered if it really was such a good idea to leave them to it, but Hannah reminded herself that ignorance was bliss. Dorothy would say what she wanted whether Hannah was there or not, and that car journey alone had proved it was better to be out of earshot.

As they pulled up outside the house, Hannah grabbed Dorothy's provisions bag that sat next to her. She got out of the car and dragging her feet as she went, made her way up the garden path to unlock the door. Heading straight for the kitchen, with Dorothy and Gabe close behind, she dumped the bag down.

She was about to go straight upstairs when Dorothy suddenly seemed to remember something important.

"I've just realised," Dorothy said. With a glint in her eye, she put a hand up to her chest in an exaggerated fashion. "I haven't spoken to your mum recently."

Hannah's heart sank. Dorothy had clearly pre-empted Hannah's plan to disappear, and this was her way of making sure Hannah and Gabe had time alone.

"I know she's been busy with the builders, but I wouldn't want Janice thinking I'm ignoring her. You're okay to put the kettle on, aren't you, Hannah, while I give her a quick call?" Without waiting for an answer, Dorothy headed out of the room.

When it came to fabricating an emergency, Hannah thought Dorothy could have at least tried to be a bit more creative. Hannah turned to Gabe and with no other choice, decided to deal with her aunt's behaviour head on. "I'm sorry. She's got it into her head we'd make a great couple."

"And you don't think we would?"

Hannah took in Gabe's earnest expression, not quite sure what to say. Despite his composure, he had to be teasing. "Why? Do you?"

"I asked first." Gabe raised an eyebrow as if waiting for an answer.

Holding his gaze, Hannah tried to figure out what was really going on in that head of his, but she felt too flustered. As if her heart hadn't had enough exercise thanks to all the walking-come-jogging she'd done that evening, her pulse raced. She turned to busy herself making the tea. "Sugar?" she asked, her voice cracking.

"Yes, please," Gabe said. "And milk."

Hearing Gabe take a seat at the table, Hannah told herself he wasn't really interested in her, he was only being playful. Granted it was a strange kind of playful, one that didn't involve laughter or banter or any kind of joke... Realising her brain was going into mentally rambling overdrive, she breathed deeply to compose herself before joining him with two mugs.

"Don't worry about Aunt Dorothy," Gabe said. "I've been getting the same from Dad. He's forever nagging me to start dating again."

Hannah noted the word *again* and wondered what lay behind it.

"In fact..." Gabe paused, as if deciding whether to continue or not.

"In fact, what?"

Gabe glanced over at the dresser, his gaze settling on the pink flowers that just about clung to life. "I didn't actually send those." He wrinkled his nose. "Dad did."

Gabe's admission was the perfect icebreaker to lift the atmosphere. Hannah couldn't help but let out a laugh. "You're kidding me."

"I wish I was."

"How did he know my address?"

"As soon as I mentioned the lion at the door, he knew exactly which house was yours. Apparently you say hello to each other when he's on his way to the cemetery to see Mum."

Hannah thought for a moment and a picture of Roger began to form. "A dapper chap? Always suited and booted? With a great head of hair?"

Gabe smiled. "That's him."

Hannah narrowed her eyes as she scrutinised Gabe's features. "I can see a resemblance now you've said it." She sniggered. "Thank goodness I didn't ring your number."

"Bet you were tempted though," Gabe said, laughing.

Hannah ignored the quip. "That does explain your weird response when I thanked you for them."

"Is that why you turned down my coffee invite?"

Like Hannah needed reminding of that. She'd regretted it ever since. "A new experience for you, was it? Getting knocked back."

"Hardly."

Having seen how Francesca and even the sports centre receptionist had responded to Gabe, Hannah didn't believe him for one second.

Gabe picked up his cup. Putting it to his lips, his eyes remained firmly on Hannah.

Butterflies wreaked havoc in Hannah's tummy. His stare wasn't just intense it seemed loaded.

"Maybe I'll ask you again sometime," Gabe said.

Hannah wondered if Gabe was flirting with her. She'd been out of the dating game so long, she'd didn't know anymore.

"You might not have to if Liv has her way," she said in answer to Gabe's question.

Gabe's expression turned quizzical.

"She thinks our team-building activity should be a group meal out, including your friend Quentin and Mel's new partner Russel."

"Ooh a triple date?" Gabe appeared to like the idea.

"Which is exactly what Liv said."

Taking a sip of her drink, Hannah suddenly panicked. It was one thing sitting in her kitchen enjoying a bit of banter with Gabe, but to hear him imply a real-life assignation was something else. "Although it isn't a date really," Hannah said. "It's a group thing. Aunt Dorothy will be there, remember."

"I should hope so. It wouldn't be the same without her."

"As long as we've got that straight." Hannah couldn't backtrack quick enough.

"Although it sounds like it's not just Aunt Dorothy who thinks we'd make a great couple," Gabe said, with a sparkle in his eyes.

Hannah wondered what his reaction would be if she called his bluff and suggested they test the theory. Feeling brave, she opened her mouth to speak, but Gabe's mobile rang, interrupting the moment.

Surprisingly, he seemed disappointed too. "Sorry," he said, rolling his eyes.

Hannah watched him pull his phone from his pocket. Discretely craning her neck, she saw the name "Kate" flash up on the screen.

Gabe's expression turned serious, and he declined the call.

"Everything okay?" Hannah asked.

"Sorry?"

Hannah indicated his mobile.

"Erm, yes. Thank you." He smiled, stuffing it back in his pocket. "Just a client."

"At this time of night?" Hannah wondered whatever happened to office hours.

"Some of them can be a bit demanding."

Hannah got up from her seat. "More tea?"

"Actually, I'm good thanks."

Gabe surprised Hannah when he too rose to his feet. "I should probably get going."

CHAPTER 29

*H*annah groaned as she got out of bed. After the previous evening's group training session, her body was stiffer than she'd anticipated. She wondered why she was putting herself through the agony. A better idea would have been to get everyone she knew to sponsor Mel and Liv. That way, the charity would still get their money and she wouldn't feel a hundred years old.

Putting on her dressing gown and making her way downstairs, Hannah heard voices in the kitchen. Recognising her mum's dulcet tones, Hannah strained to hear what she and Aunt Dorothy were talking about but she couldn't decipher the conversation. Wondering what her mum could possibly want at that time of the morning, Hannah sighed, supposing she was about to find out.

"Morning," Hannah said as she entered the kitchen.

Janice and Dorothy sat at the table enjoying a cup of tea.

"How are you feeling today?" Dorothy asked, rising to her feet to make Hannah a cuppa.

Hannah gently lowered herself into a chair. "Sore."

"Aunt Dorothy was just telling me about your running antics," Janice said. "I must say I'm surprised you've stuck with it."

"I wish I hadn't."

Janice laughed. "Well, you were warned."

Recalling her mum's less-than-encouraging response when Hannah had first mentioned the race, the last thing she needed was an *I told you so*.

"Janice, I'm surprised at you," Dorothy said, clearly offended. "She might not look up to much this morning, but Hannah's doing really well." Dorothy expression relaxed. "Here you go." She placed Hannah's mug on the table and took a seat.

"Ha!" Hannah couldn't help herself. "You think?"

"I most certainly do."

Hannah appreciated the vote of confidence, even if her aunt's definition of *really well* didn't reflect reality.

"Aunt Dorothy also tells me that gorgeous cyclist of a man is helping you train," Janice said. Her eager eyes belied her nonchalant tone.

"He is."

Her mum was so transparent. Before Janice next opened her mouth Hannah knew where their conversation was going.

"So it's not all doom and gloom then." Janice paused, her eyebrow raised. "And how are you both getting on?"

Hannah pictured Dorothy on the phone to her mum the previous evening, easily imagining their frantic discussion about flower deliveries, coffee dates, and Dorothy's not-so-creative manoeuvre to ensure Hannah and Gabe had some alone time. Hannah was surprised their excitement hadn't caused an electric storm in the airwaves. "That's why you're here, is it? To get the gossip?"

Ignoring Hannah's quip, Janice sipped on her tea. "And I believe he sent you flowers?"

Looking from Janice to Dorothy and back again, Hannah thought the two women were as bad as each other. She didn't have the heart to explain that the flowers hadn't come from Gabe at all, but rather his dad. She glanced over at the dresser. Once a profusion of pinks and purple, the blooms had faded, wilted, and dried. Their stems appeared as brittle as Hannah's over-exercised joints felt. "If you already know, why are you asking?"

"Is there anything else you'd like to share?" Janice asked.

As Dorothy and Janice stared at Hannah, their eyes wide in eager anticipation, she recalled Gabe's phone ringing, the name Kate flashing up on the screen, and how he'd quickly declined the call rather than answer. She fixed a smile on her face. "Nope."

Dorothy and Janice slumped in their seats.

"Well, you *will* ask," Hannah said, laughing.

"There's nothing wrong with me showing an interest in your life, Hannah."

"Great. I take it that means you'll be sponsoring me in the charity race."

Janice seemed surprised Hannah had to ask. "Of course I'll sponsor you." She rose to her feet. "Right, I should get going. Those builders have been left to their own devices for long enough."

"I'll see you out," Dorothy said.

Hannah scoffed. They were clearly about to have another conflab about Hannah's non-existent love life.

Hannah wrapped her hands around her mug and raising it to her lips, took a sip. She reflected on the previous evening and the mixed messages she'd got from Gabe. One minute, he was flirting with her and talking about triple dates, something Hannah had to admit she found both scary *and* heaven-sent. Then in the next, Gabe couldn't seem to get out of there quickly enough.

Hannah took a deep breath and exhaled. She didn't think she'd ever met such a contradictory man.

CHAPTER 30

*G*abe sat cross-legged at the foot of his mother's grave. He picked at the tufts of grass next to his feet, which were already short, thanks to the care Gabe's dad took looking after the plot.

Roger kept a simple push-along mower in the boot of his car especially for the job and he made sure to keep up a rotation of fresh flowers in the grave vase. Of course, there were paid groundsmen about the place, whose job it was to keep the cemetery looking respectable. But that didn't stop Roger applying his own personal touch.

Setting out for a walk, Gabe hadn't planned on visiting his mum, but as was usual when he had something on his mind, he'd gone into automatic pilot and found himself meandering along the cemetery pathways until suddenly he'd reached her final resting place.

Lifting his gaze, he stared at the headstone and not for the first time wished it was her sat opposite instead of a huge engraved slab of marble. He wanted to see her riant brown eyes glisten with curiosity and intelligence as she talked to him about life, art, history, or whatever she had on her mind.

He wanted to watch her laughter lines deepen as she threw her head back and guffawed uncontrollably at a joke only she understood. But more than anything, Gabe wanted to feel his mum's arms around him and hear her comforting words of wisdom.

He could have talked to his dad, but rather than being a sounding board Roger was a man who sprang into action and not always with Gabe's approval. The bouquet of flowers he'd sent to Hannah being a prime example.

"You'd like her, Mum," Gabe said. "She's funny and smart and I know you'll call me shallow when I say this, but she's beautiful too." Picturing Hannah, he couldn't help but sigh. "She's the whole package, all right."

"You're quite a catch yourself," he heard his mum say.

Gabe scoffed. Like most mums, his was biased. Even in death it seemed.

His smile faded. If his mum was sat on a cloud looking down on him, encouraging him during the good times and supporting him through the bad, she also knew the reason he was holding back.

"Talk to her, Gabe. Tell her how you feel."

The previous evening played out in his head. "I almost did, Mum." When Hannah had joked about everyone thinking they'd make a great couple, Gabe had been so close to admitting he thought that too.

"Then what stopped you?" his mum asked.

That was something Gabe himself had been questioning from the second he'd chickened out. "Who knows?"

He pictured his mum wearing the exact expression she'd always used whenever he had cause to be evasive. Lips pursed and brows raised, her eyes drilled into him.

Gabe relented. "Because the moment passed. Because she might not feel the same about me and I didn't want to scare her away." He fell silent for a moment. "Because she might feel *exactly* the same and then I'd have to…" His voice trailed off.

"Explain?"

Gabe nodded.

"Sounds to me like you're the one who's frightened."

Gabe let out a laugh. "Of course I bloody am."

He could still feel the sudden panic he felt when he saw the name *Kate* flash up on his phone screen. He couldn't believe after all that time her details were still on his contact list. Gabe chewed on the inside of his cheek, embarrassed by his own behaviour. "I lied to Hannah, Mum. I lied. And then I did a runner."

Staring at her headstone, he wondered if his mum was as disappointed in her son, as her son was in himself.

CHAPTER 31

*A*s Hannah let herself into the house, it seemed being hot, sweaty and bright red had become her new norm. From the moment she realised she was the weakest runner on the team, she'd made a point of getting out every day to improve her performance. An accomplishment she'd unfortunately yet to achieve.

"I'm back," she called out, so Aunt Dorothy could stop the clock. Hannah took off Archie's baseball cap and tossing it to one side, headed for the kitchen. She plonked herself down on a chair. "How did I do?"

Dorothy passed her the record sheet.

Hannah frowned as she read. "I don't understand. I'm doing everything right. Walking, jogging, walking… Just like we did in the group session. Surely I should be a lot faster by now." She pulled out her phone and checked her step count. "Apparently, the average number of steps for a 5k run is 6,250." Hannah held her phone up for Dorothy to see. "Look, at the rate I'm going, the organisers will have packed up and gone home by the time I cross the finish line."

Dorothy sympathised. "How long do you get?"

"An hour." Hannah sighed. "I really wanted a medal too."

"There has to be something you can do," Dorothy said, clearly seeing the dilemma.

"Such as?"

Dorothy's eyes lit up. "What about getting one of those treadmills?"

Hannah straightened up in her seat. "You know what, you're a genius. If I had one of those, I could push myself more not just on speed but distance. Instead of automatically slowing down when I get tired, I'll have to keep going."

Dorothy laughed. "You will if you don't want to fly off the end."

Hannah picked up her phone again. Hitting the internet, she decided to research the kinds of running machines available. Her excitement waned. "That's that then. They're far too expensive."

"Maybe Gabe can help. He might know of someone who could lend you one."

"You think? I suppose I could ask. He is a fitness freak. And I'd only need it for a couple of weeks."

"Unless you want to keep up your training after the race is over."

Hannah flashed her aunt an amused look. "I think we both know that's not going to happen." Getting up from her seat, Hannah headed over to the dresser and opening a drawer, pulled out the florist's card she'd hidden away that had come with Gabe's dad's flower delivery.

She typed a text on her phone and keyed in Gabe's telephone number, before hitting send. Surprised to hear it bleep almost immediately, Hannah smiled as she read Gabe's response. "How's that for service? He'll have one here within the hour." Hannah glanced around, excited. "Now to decide where to put it."

"How about in the lounge? There'll be plenty of room if you move the sofa."

"That could work," Hannah said, happy to give it a try.

With Dorothy's help, Hannah spent the following forty-five minutes preparing for the treadmill's arrival. Moving the sofa and coffee table out of the way, she made sure the television could be seen from where the running machine would sit, while at the same time ensuring Dorothy's viewing wasn't affected.

Back in the kitchen, Hannah had dug out her earphones and after some serious consideration, she and Dorothy had put together the perfect running playlist.

"I can't wait to try these out," Hannah said of the music they'd chosen. Her phone rang and she checked the screen. "It's Beth and Archie."

"You go ahead," Dorothy said. "I'll keep Gabe busy if he turns up sooner than planned."

Appreciative, Hannah headed into the lounge and settling herself on the repositioned sofa, clicked to answer. "Hello, you two."

"What's happened to the living room?" Beth asked, bemused.

"It looks different," Archie said.

Beth narrowed her eyes. "*You* look different."

Hannah had to admit that since her evening banter with Gabe, she *felt* different. For fifteen years she'd been known as Janice's daughter, Beth and Archie's mum, or Carl's wife, and subsequently ex-wife. Somewhere along the line she'd lost who she was in her own right. Gabe's penetrating gaze might have caused her insides to somersault, but it had also made her feel like Hannah the woman, something she didn't just find nerve-wracking, she found it liberating.

"I've moved some furniture around to make room for a treadmill."

"Really?" Beth said. "You are taking this sponsored run seriously."

Archie looked impressed. "That's brilliant."

"So what have you two been up to?" Hannah asked.

"We visited Aix-en-Provence the other day."

"Ah, Paul Cézanne territory. Did you check out his studio?"

"The Atelier Cézanne. Yes, we did," Beth proudly replied.

"Excellent." Hannah was pleased to see on that occasion her children weren't hitting Google to do a knowledge check.

"It's a nice place, but I'm in no rush to go back," Archie said. "It was all museums and fountains."

Hannah stared at her son, horrified. "You can't say that. Aix-en-Provence is rich in history and culture."

"Which is great if you like that kind of thing," Archie replied.

A knock at the front door caught Hannah's attention. She heard Dorothy pass by and a second later welcome Gabe. Hannah wanted to clap her hands in excitement. She couldn't believe she felt enthusiastic about a piece of exercise equipment, especially one that involved running.

Gabe popped his head into the room. "Everything all right."

Hannah spun round. "Yes. Why wouldn't it be?"

"No reason." A smile spread across Gabe's face and giving her a wink, he disappeared again.

"Who's that?" Beth and Archie chorused.

Turning back to her children, Hannah felt herself blush. "My personal trainer," she said, trying to keep her voice light.

"You have a PT?" Archie asked. "Go, Mum!"

Unlike her brother, Beth appeared less than impressed.

"He's here to deliver the treadmill I mentioned," Hannah explained.

"He gives all his clients a wink like that, does he?" Beth asked.

Not realising Gabe had been seen on screen, Hannah took in her daughter's indignation. "I couldn't say. I've never seen him with any of his other clients."

"Does he have a name?" Archie asked.

"Yes. His name's Gabe."

"Whose name is Gabe?" Joining Beth and Archie, Carl had clearly got over his sulking.

"Mum's personal trainer. He just winked at her," Archie said.

Carl frowned. "That doesn't sound right. What kind of professional behaves like that?"

"It's only an eye movement," Hannah said, wondering why the fuss.

"He fancies her," Archie carried on.

"He does not," Hannah said.

"I think Mum fancies him too," Beth said, as if Hannah hadn't spoken. "I get why. For an older man he doesn't look bad. Anyway, that's why she's defending him. And probably why she seems different. See." Beth indicated Carl make a proper assessment of Hannah. "She's all happy and her eyes are brighter."

"It's about time she showed interest in someone," Archie said. "I mean I'm glad she's not like you, Dad. Let's face it, until Monica came along, it was a new woman almost every week."

Carl stared at his son with a mix of shock and offence. "I wouldn't go that far."

Beth and Archie gave him a knowing look. "Really?" they said.

Archie nudged his sister. "Think about it. She might stop fussing over us now."

"I'll believe that when I see it," Carl said, laughing.

Hannah stared at her children and ex-husband. "Excuse me. I *am* still here, you know."

Gabe entered the room with a cup of tea in hand. "Aunt Dorothy sent me in with this."

Hannah smiled on the outside and cringed on the in. Questioning why Dorothy would do that, Hannah hoped to goodness Gabe hadn't heard what had just been said. "Thank you." She willed him to beat a retreat.

Handing the tea over, Gabe glanced at Hannah's phone screen. "Hello," he said to Beth, Archie, and Carl.

"Hello again," Beth and Archie replied, while Carl puffed his chest out and gave Gabe a curt nod.

"Didn't I tell you he's good looking," Beth said to her dad.

"Nice to meet you all," Gabe said. He turned his attention to

Hannah. "I'll leave you to it." Giving her another wink, he chuckled as he headed out the way he'd come.

Hannah's stomach sank like it was tied to a block of concrete. Gabe might not have heard every word, but he'd clearly heard enough.

"Kids," Carl said. "Why don't you go and get ready. I wouldn't mind a word with your mum."

"We're spending the afternoon at the beach," Beth said to Hannah.

"Dad and Monica want a lazy day," Archie said.

"I can think of worse things than an afternoon in the French sunshine," Hannah said. "Think of me while you're both having fun." She waited until the kids were out of earshot before speaking again. "If this is so you can tell me to be careful you needn't worry. Not only am I a grown woman, there's nothing–"

"It's not. I wanted to..." Carl took a deep breath. "I just thought you should..."

Watching him struggle to find the right words, Hannah didn't think she'd seen Carl so flustered. Wondering what he could possibly be trying to say, Hannah's mind went into overdrive, conjuring up various worst-case scenarios. "Are you sick? Have the kids done something wrong?" *Oh, Lordy*. She put a hand up to cover her mouth, trying not to giggle. "Monica's not pregnant, is she?"

"No, she's not!" The thought of being a dad for a third time clearly wasn't a thought Carl relished. "But I am going to ask her to marry me."

Falling silent, Hannah's eyes widened in surprise.

"I've chartered a catamaran for a couple of days. You know, to make it memorable."

Hannah continued to stare.

"Sunset on the horizon, crew at the ready with champagne to hand, me down on one knee..."

Hannah recalled the night Carl had proposed to her. It

involved a Chinese takeout and a bottle of Cava. Dumbstruck by what she was hearing, Hannah wondered if she should ask for an increase in child support. Unlike back in the day, the man clearly had money to burn.

Carl returned her gaze, as if expecting a response.

Hannah's shocked silence continued.

"Please say something, Hannah."

Trying to find the right words, Hannah swallowed hard. She gave Carl an over-the-top smile. "Congratulations."

CHAPTER 32

*H*annah had thought she'd never see the day when Carl committed for a second time. Experience had taught her he wasn't the marrying kind. Telling herself that Monica must be one special lady, Hannah entered the kitchen in a bit of a daze.

Sat at the dining table with Gabe, Aunt Dorothy looked up. "Everything all right?"

"Carl's just informed me he wants to get married," Hannah said.

Gabe scraped his chair back. "Shall I go and start setting up the treadmill?" he asked, as if such a conversation was none of his business.

"No," Hannah replied. "Please. Finish your tea first."

Sitting back down again, Gabe's discomfort was obvious.

"How do you feel about that?" Dorothy asked.

"To be honest, I'm a bit shocked," Hannah replied. "Not about the proposal, as such." She recalled the day Carl had taken Beth and Archie to France. "He had something on his mind a couple of weeks ago. He wanted to talk to me back then, but in the end decided not to."

"Then what is it? Because something's bothering you."

"He's hired a catamaran. With a crew. For a couple of days." Hannah glanced around the room, taking in her beautiful but bargain-because-needs-must possessions. "How much money does that man have?"

Dorothy laughed. "What do Beth and Archie think?"

"About Carl's wallet?"

"No, the proposal."

"They don't know yet. Carl didn't want them blurting it out without speaking to me first." Hannah shrugged. "I can't see it being an issue though. By all accounts they get on well with Monica."

"It was good of him to let you know," Dorothy said.

"I suppose." Hannah scoffed. "Although knowing Carl, he'll have expected a few dramatics on my part. As his ex, I'd of course be jealous."

"Maybe I should go and come back later," Gabe said, his discomfort increasing. "You've obviously got stuff to talk about."

Hannah let out a laugh. "Not at all." She dismissed his concern with a wave of her hand. "Really, his engagement isn't an issue. Carl and I have been divorced since forever." She thought for a moment. "I suppose if I'm truthful, I'm feeling a bit jealous. I can't imagine anyone wanting to charter a boat for me."

"Really. I *should* leave you to it."

Appreciating Gabe's concern, Hannah took a deep breath. "Believe me, everything's fine." Putting all thoughts of glamorous sailing vessels out of her mind once and for all, she rose to her feet. "Although you're probably right about this treadmill of yours. We should get it sorted."

After helping to bring it in from the car, Hannah sat on the sofa arm watching Gabe assemble the running machine. Studying him, she questioned how he managed to continue looking handsome despite his concentration. Whenever Hannah had cause to focus like that, it invariably involved screwing up her face and sticking her tongue out.

She took in his mass of dark hair and half-tempted to reach out and run her hands through it, she wondered what Gabe's story was. That's if he had one, she supposed. Gabe had said so little about himself, it was hard to tell. He most certainly knew more about her than she did him. Unsurprisingly so, Hannah reasoned. Thinking back to when she'd collided with Gabe's bike and her subsequent meltdown, Hannah couldn't deny she'd overshared somewhat.

She sighed as Gabe continued to work, glad of his help. Technical, physical, emotional, whatever needed sorting out, Hannah usually had no choice but to get on with it herself. She thought back to the day Dorothy had arrived, remembering what her mum had said about how, instead of running around after everyone else, Hannah should enjoy being the recipient for a change. For once, her mum had been right. Although on the downside, getting her head into gear once the kids were back and life returned to normal wasn't a challenge Hannah looked forward to.

Gabe suddenly stopped what he was doing. "What?" He'd clearly felt Hannah's eyes on him.

"I'm just admiring your concentration."

Seeing him shake his head and get back to it, Hannah felt guilty for not being truthful with Gabe earlier. She hadn't lied when she said she was fine with Carl asking Monica to marry him. But she hadn't been one hundred per cent honest either.

It wasn't Carl's announcement that bothered her; Hannah genuinely wished Carl and Monica well. There were just so many changes taking place and Carl's engagement plan was yet something else Hannah had to deal with. Liv, Mel, Carl, they were all moving on in their lives. Things for Hannah, on the other hand, remained stagnant.

"Penny for them," Gabe said.

Snapping out of her reverie, Hannah had been so lost in her own thoughts she was surprised to see the treadmill ready to go. She indicated his handiwork. "I was thinking I can't wait to get started."

Gabe rose to his feet. "Then let me talk you through the various settings, and you'll be good to go." Turning his attention to the LCD screen, he explained what Hannah needed to know.

"I think I can remember that," she said, once Gabe had finished.

Gabe's phone rang and watching him pull it out of his pocket, Hannah was convinced she caught the name Kate on the screen.

Looking harassed, Gabe declined the call and seeming to block the number, he shoved the phone away again.

Curious, Hannah wondered who the mystery woman was. The fact that Gabe refused to speak to her showed there was more to his and Kate's connection than he was letting on. But having snooped over his shoulder, it wasn't as if Hannah could question him about that direct. "The demanding client?" she asked instead.

"Something like that."

Much to Hannah's frustration, he refused to say any more about it and moved straight on.

"I've put together a workout schedule." Producing a sheet of paper, he unfolded it and handed it to Hannah. "Starting now, it takes you right up to race day."

Hannah read what he'd written. She looked to Gabe confused. "But this says I only need to train four days a week."

"It does. When it comes to any kind of exercise routine, time off is just as important. It gives your body and brain the chance to recharge. Believe me, they need that recovery time."

Hannah continued to study the sheet. She let out a laugh. "You really think I'll be running a full 2.5k come Saturday? In one go? No stopping or walking?" She wrinkled her nose in disbelief. "In an hour or less?"

"I don't see why not. You've been doing great the last couple of weeks."

Hannah looked at him like he'd gone mad. "You saw the speed Mel and Francesca ran at." Hannah still hadn't got over being lapped. "Even Liv got fed up with my slow pace and left me to it."

As Gabe returned her gaze, there was a sincerity in his eyes. "Trust me. You've got this."

Hannah's face lit up. Bolstered by Gabe's encouragement, after all he was the expert, she began to believe that herself.

CHAPTER 33

Sitting at the table with a healing cup of tea, Gabe glanced over at his vehicle keys hanging on the hook by the kitchen door. It would have been easy to grab them, jump in his car, and head round to Hannah's. It wasn't as if he didn't have a valid reason. Having organised the treadmill on Hannah's behalf, it was logical for him to check in to see how she was coping with it. She might even need advice on the training schedule he'd put together.

However, having decided to give Hannah some space, Gabe resisted the urge. Recalling her response upon hearing the news that her ex-husband hoped to remarry, Gabe thought the last thing Hannah needed was him hanging around. Hannah might have said she and Carl were long over and even joked about no one ever chartering a boat for her, but once the news sank in Carl's moving on could have stirred up memories of what the two of them once shared. Hannah could be thinking about what she'd lost and what might have been.

Or you could be using Carl's situation as an excuse, Gabe's inner voice suggested. *To stop yourself getting in too deep.*

Gabe let out a laugh. "It's a bit late for that, don't you think?"

He couldn't believe a woman, whom he'd met less than three weeks prior, had made such an impact on him and sitting there, he had to wonder what was wrong with Carl. If Gabe was ever lucky enough to be in a relationship with Hannah, he couldn't imagine any good reason to leave her.

His loss is your gain, the little voice said.

"You think?" Gabe replied. As far as he was concerned, he was a long way from that.

Gabe sighed. He'd had the perfect opportunity to tell Hannah how he felt, but instead of being honest, he'd chickened out and let the moment pass. He might not be ready to declare undying love for Hannah, but he could have said he agreed with everyone else in that they'd make a great couple. He pictured the scene. Him asking her for her thoughts on the matter. Hannah asking him for his. Neither of them daring to give a straight answer. He shook his head and sighed. The two of them were clearly as bad as each other.

Gabe cocked his head, as a thought suddenly struck him. "Hannah didn't disagree." Gabe let out a laugh, wondering why he hadn't realised that at the time. Maybe there was hope, after all?

He glanced over at his car keys once more, but again suppressed the lure to go and see Hannah. It wasn't as if Carl's situation had changed. He was still moving on and Hannah might still have stuff to deal with. The white envelope Gabe continued to ignore caught his eye, reminding him that Hannah wasn't the only one with an ex to get around.

He stared at the envelope. Whatever it was Kate wanted from him, Gabe knew from old there was drama ahead.

CHAPTER 34

"*I*'m looking forward to this," Aunt Dorothy said.

So was Hannah. It was one of her rest days and with no stretching, jiggling, and running to get on with, she was determined to make the most of it.

Dorothy's happiness continued, as they pulled onto the car park. "I can't remember the last time I was treated to lunch out."

Their trip into town was twofold. Not only were they having a team meeting, Hannah wanted to say thank you to Dorothy for all she'd done the last couple of weeks. "I hope you're hungry," Hannah said, as they unclipped their seat belts, climbed out of the vehicle and set off down the street.

"Perhaps we could do a little window shopping when we're done? Or even indulge ourselves? She indicated Hannah's attire. "You look like you need some new clothes."

Hannah inched up her jeans as she walked. "I think you might be right."

Dorothy's enthusiasm continued all the way to the little bistro. "This is very nice." She paused before entering to admire the restaurant's olde worlde signage and to read the A-board that hinted at the menu on offer. "It says here they do continental-style lunches, whatever that means."

Hannah smiled, imagining Dorothy later that evening. Hannah knew her aunt would regale Uncle Denis with a detailed account of the fun she was, no doubt, about to have. Hannah pulled on the heavy glass door. "You ready?" She gestured for Dorothy to enter first.

Hannah had never visited that restaurant before either and she was impressed with its terracotta, mustard and olive-green colour palette. Chandeliers hung from old wooden beams that Hannah would have put money on being original, and dining tables sat on a natural tiled floor.

"Beautiful," Dorothy said, echoing Hannah's thoughts. She glanced around. "Now, where's the rest of the team?"

Mel and Liv waved at them from a table situated in the far corner.

"There they are." Hastening over, Dorothy led the way.

After hugs all round, Liv wolf-whistled at Dorothy, admiring her from head to toe. "Look at you." She indicated Dorothy's floral cotton summer dress. "That's gorgeous."

Dorothy blushed. "What, this old thing," she said, as everyone took a seat.

Mel cocked her head at Hannah's choice of wardrobe. "Have you lost weight?"

Hannah glanced down at her baggier-than-usual jeans and too-loose-fitting blouse. She pictured herself sweating as she pushed herself through the pain barrier on the running machine. "The *only* perk of Gabe's training regime, I have to say. Every time I get on it I think I'm gonna die. Then again, ever since I met him, the man's been wanting to kill me."

"He's been wanting to do something to you," Dorothy said. "And believe me it's not that."

Mel and Liv burst out laughing, while Hannah flushed red. "Aunt Dorothy!"

"And that cuts both ways, no matter what you claim, young lady."

Liv leaned towards Dorothy. "I agree," she said, still chuckling.

Mel swallowed her amusement. "So the training's going well then?"

"It is," Hannah replied, glad to be moving the conversation on.

"And what about your breathing? Have you mastered that?"

Hannah nodded. Compared to her prior puffing and panting, the "in through the nose and out through the mouth" method had become second nature. "I have."

"She's doing really well since getting the treadmill. You've improved your times brilliantly, haven't you, Hannah?" Dorothy beamed with pride. "Of course, the real test will be at the weekend."

"Don't remind me," Hannah said. She might have built up her stamina on the jogging front, but she still incorporated periodic walks into her session. "Just the thought of running 2.5k in one go makes me nervous."

"According to Gabe," Dorothy said. "She'll be blasting the 5k come race day no problem."

"That's a bit of an exaggeration." Not once had Hannah heard the word *blasting* leave Gabe's mouth.

Showing her competitive side, Mel clapped her hands, happy to hear it regardless. "This team is so going to smash this race."

Liv handed out menus. "Unlike you two ladies of leisure, Mel and I have to clock watch. So, what are we all having?"

Hannah scoffed. "Ladies of leisure? I wish." Hannah might not have had Beth and Archie to run around after of late, but she certainly hadn't lain on the sofa reading books while dropping chocolates into her mouth as intended. What was meant to have been a time for relaxation, had seemed anything but. Emotionally and physically, she was beginning to wear out. "How is work?" Hannah asked, as she scanned the food on offer.

"The same as always," Mel replied. "You're not missing much."

"Talking of the team, how are we all fixed for this Saturday. I hope you don't mind, but I've booked a table at that fancy Italian that's just opened."

Hannah let her menu drop. "I thought you had a rally to attend on Saturday."

"That's a day thing. We'll easily be back in time to join you come evening."

"Now we have no excuse," Dorothy said to Hannah. "After lunch, we're definitely hitting the shops."

Liv sighed. "I can't wait for you all to meet Quentin."

"Will Russel be joining us too?" Dorothy asked, her eyes bright with anticipation.

"Ooh, yes," Hannah said. "Tell us how your video call went? Is Russel as chatty in person as he is on a keyboard?"

Mel's smile faded. "I wouldn't know."

Hannah looked at her friend, concerned. "What do you mean?"

"There was a problem with his camera, so we're still having to make do with messaging. He was very apologetic about it."

Not apologetic enough to go out and buy a plug-in webcam, Hannah considered. Wondering if the picture she'd seen of Russel was anyone but, she reached over and rubbed Mel's arm.

"I'll ask him about Saturday night though. But remember he does live down in the Midlands, so getting here might be too much of a trek."

Hannah wondered, if in making his excuses before she'd even asked, Mel was already trying to cushion her disappointment.

"I'm sure he'll jump at the chance to meet you face to face," Dorothy said, ever the optimist.

Hannah wrinkled her nose. "What about Francesca? Should we invite her too? I mean, technically she is part of the team."

"For what it's worth, I think we should," Dorothy said.

A part of Hannah wished she hadn't asked. "You do?"

"I appreciate Francesca isn't the easiest of people," Dorothy said. "But underneath all that bravado, she's probably like the rest of us; insecure."

That was not a characteristic Hannah would have ascribed to Francesca.

"I mean, she obviously thinks she has something to prove," Dorothy said. "Why else would she behave the way she does?"

Hannah contemplated Francesca's competitiveness, not just in how she performed but also in how she looked. The woman was forever preening herself to make sure her appearance stayed perfect. Hannah had never seen Francesca with a hair out of place or a crease in her clothes.

Realising her aunt might have a point, Hannah suddenly felt guilty. Seeing Francesca more as a nuisance, Hannah had never tried to appreciate what might lie behind the woman's façade. Not once had it crossed her mind that Francesca's overconfidence might be masking a lack of it.

"Thankfully, it's not an issue," Liv said.

As bad as Hannah felt, she couldn't deny her relief.

"She's busy on Saturday night." Mel sniffed. "Unlike the rest of us who couldn't get tickets, Francesca is off to the Danny Parkes concert."

Liv grimaced. "Don't we know it. She hasn't stopped banging on about it for days."

"Now, now, ladies," Dorothy said.

Liv turned to Hannah. "So, how are things with Gabe?" she asked, moving the conversation on.

Hannah had thought they'd already discussed that. "When you say *with*?"

"I'm just wondering if you've seen him lately? How he's doing? You know."

Hannah considered Liv as bad as Dorothy and aware that her friend was making more than a general enquiry, that she was fishing for something juicy, Hannah shrugged. "How would I know? Maybe you should speak to Quentin, what with him and Gabe being friends?"

Dorothy sighed, her disappointment on the matter evident. "We haven't seen Gabe since Hannah got her treadmill."

Hannah couldn't deny she'd been a tad disappointed too. She'd expected him to at least check up on how she was getting on with the running machine and specially devised training programme. She wondered if his mystery woman had anything to do with him going AWOL. More to the point, she wondered who the mystery woman was.

It would have been easy for Hannah to drop Kate into the conversation. After all, Liv would run straight back to Quentin to get the dirt and relay it back. But as much as Hannah's curiosity was trying to get the better of her, she knew she had to ignore it. The last thing she wanted was to cause unnecessary strain on Liv's relationship with Quentin. Or, indeed, on Quentin and Gabe's friendship. That simply wouldn't be fair.

"You know what they say, Aunt Dorothy," Liv said. "Absence makes the heart grow fonder."

"Not on my part it doesn't," Hannah said, trying to maintain an air of coolness.

Dorothy, Mel and Liv all raised their eyebrows. "You're sure about that?"

CHAPTER 35

*S*afely back at their villa, Beth and Archie video called. While keen to find out how Carl's marriage proposal had gone, Hannah didn't want to appear too eager. Suppressing her enthusiasm, she knew Beth and Archie would get to it when they were ready. "So how was your sailing trip?" Hannah asked. Feet up on the sofa, she settled herself to hear all about it.

"The catamaran was very posh," Beth said. "It had two deck areas. One had a canopy and was taken up by seating and a dining table."

"The other was open air and it had these mats laid out for sunbathing," Archie said.

Hannah fake smiled, trying to look interested as she waited for them to get to the good bits.

"Inside was decorated in beiges, whites and greys."

"The cabins were a bit small. Although very nice."

"And the beds were comfy."

As she listened to them, Hannah wondered what was wrong with her children. It was one thing having to wait to hear all about Carl's engagement, but they could have at least told her about their lazy mornings spent lounging under the sun, and afternoon swimming sessions in a never-ending crystal blue sea.

They could have let Hannah delight in the gorgeous cuisine they'd experienced, such as Daube Provençale, Fougasse smeared with Pissaladière, and Tarte Tropézienne. All cooked and served by charming and handsome French crew members. The last thing Hannah anticipated was some boring accommodation critique. Beth and Archie sounded so dispassionate about their boat trip, Hannah could almost hear the *but* that was about to follow.

Their faces fell and Hannah raised her eyebrows in readiness.

"We got seasick," they said.

Hannah put a hand up to hide her mouth. She knew she shouldn't laugh. Motion sickness was soul destroying. However, the waters between the South of France and Corsica at that time of year weren't known for being choppy and Hannah swallowed, trying to stop her voice cracking. "You poor things."

"It was awful," Beth said.

"I've never felt so ill," Archie said.

"But you must have something positive to say about your trip," Hannah said. If nothing else, there was Carl's engagement to talk about.

"We spent a day on Corsica."

Hannah perked up. "That must have been nice."

"But we couldn't enjoy it. By the time the nausea had gone we had to get back on the catamaran."

As much as Hannah empathised, she had thought Beth and Archie were made of sterner stuff. "Did Dad and Monica enjoy themselves?" Hannah asked, still waiting for the gossip.

Clearly onto her, her children shook their heads in disdain.

"You're so transparent, Mum," Beth said.

"Dad told us he gave you the heads-up about asking Monica to marry him," Archie said. "We knew you'd be desperate to know how it went."

"So the seasickness story was made up?" Hannah looked back at them, shocked they'd do that to her. "To teach me a lesson for being nosey?"

Beth and Archie appeared horrified.

"Oh, no, we were sick all right," Beth said.

Archie scowled. "I'm never getting on a boat again."

Hannah tried not to laugh. "So, what did Monica say?"

Beth's expression softened. "Her answer was yes."

Hannah waited for them to continue.

"If you want the details, Mum, you're gonna have to ask Dad," Archie said.

Hannah pouted. "Why can't you tell me?" She didn't even try to hide her disappointment.

Beth frowned at her mum. "Because we were holed up in bed when he proposed."

"Trying not to throw up," Archie added.

"So you were still on the catamaran at the time? Poorly? And your dad carried on with his plans, instead of taking you back to shore?" Hannah pictured Carl and Monica out at sea watching the sun go down, Carl dropping to one knee, then pulling out a ring box from his pocket and opening it up. She saw Monica's eyes brighten as tears of joy threatened. An ice-bucket, home to a bottle of champagne, sat to one side in readiness. All to the sound of her children retching in their cabins. What kind of monster was he?

"I can tell you the ring Dad gave her is an absolute rock," Beth said.

"Nothing like the piddly thing he got for you," Archie said.

Not only had Hannah never been one for big showy jewellery, she knew she'd always have a soft spot for her little engagement ring. Its diamond might've been small and the gold band it was set into thin, but when Carl had given it to her, it was the sentiment that counted. At the time, that ring had meant as much to Hannah as Monica's boulder, no doubt, meant to her. Hannah simply hoped Carl's second attempt at marriage would turn out to be more successful.

"Maybe you'll do better second time round and get a rock too?" Beth said.

Hannah frowned. "What do you mean? Who says I want to get married again?"

"That's what we want to talk to you about." Archie straightened himself up in his seat. "We've been discussing things, haven't we, Beth?"

Beth nodded.

Archie carried on. "And we think it's time for you to start dating."

"That's if you're not already," Beth said. "I mean, you and that Gabe chap seem to be getting a bit pally."

Hannah let out a laugh. She couldn't believe what she was hearing.

"Please, Mum, we're being serious here," Archie said.

Hannah immediately fell quiet. The two of them might still be teenagers, but they were evidently trying to have a grown-up conversation. It was only fair she listened to them. "I'm sorry. Please, continue."

"We don't think it's fair that Dad's had all these girlfriends and now gets to marry Monica," Beth said. "While you're stuck looking after us."

Beth's words horrified Hannah. "What do you mean? I'm not stuck with anyone." She immediately regretted letting Carl take Beth and Archie to France. The man had clearly been putting ideas in their heads. "You're my children. Not only do I love you, I'd do anything for you."

"We get that, Mum. But take your boat comment just now," Archie said. "You really would have missed out on one of the biggest moments of your life because we felt sick."

"Not any old sick," Hannah reminded them. "You were seasick."

"And what about that Uncle Denis you mentioned?" Beth said. "He was obviously important to you, but you didn't get to go to his funeral because you were too busy thinking of us."

As much as Hannah appreciated what they were saying, she couldn't say she liked it. "I'm your mum. That's my job."

Hannah hadn't lied to Aunt Dorothy when she'd said she used her business degree to its full effect as a parent. Since the day Beth and Archie were born, she'd taken everything she'd learned and efficiently fine-tuned every task that came with raising children, doing up and running a house, all the while maintaining a full-time job. She'd adapted and re-perfected what had to be done every time needs and circumstances changed.

The three of them often joked about Hannah running their day-to-day lives and home in the same way a company director ran a firm. The one thing they'd never done was complain about it. "Has someone put you up to this?" Hannah asked. Carl had always been a more relaxed parent and often thought Hannah over the top. "Has your dad said something? Has Monica?"

"No, Mum," Beth said. "This is coming from us."

"It's not as if we're babies anymore," Archie said. "It's time we started doing stuff for ourselves."

"And it's time you started doing things for *your*self," Beth added.

Hannah knew they had a point. Admittedly, similar thoughts *had* been running through her own head of late.

Archie took a deep breath and exhaled. "I'm sorry to say this, Mum, but as of today you're no longer the family CEO."

Hannah felt proud of her children for having the maturity to recognise she needed a life separate to them. "You're making me redundant?"

"See it more as going part-time," Beth said.

It might've felt like Beth and Archie had been gone forever, but it had only been three weeks. In that short time, however, they seemed to have grown not just physically, but emotionally too. Taking in their earnestness, as much as she wanted to Hannah couldn't deny they were right. The fact that they were even having that conversation with her proved Beth and Archie were ready for more responsibility.

Hannah smiled to herself, knowing they'd probably been ready for a while. She just hadn't wanted to admit it.

CHAPTER 36

"What do you mean, you've been arrested?" Although it wasn't the first time Liv had surprised her of late, that was the last thing Hannah expected to hear.

Hannah didn't usually answer calls from withheld numbers, but on that occasion something in her gut had told her she needed to. Hearing Liv's panic, Hannah was glad she'd listened to her intuition.

"A fight broke out at the rally," Liv said. "It was nothing to do with us but the police wouldn't listen, and they rounded us up anyway. We've been searched and they've taken all our belongings."

Hannah turned to Dorothy, who clearly wondered what was going on. "It's Liv," Hannah whispered. "There's been some trouble at the rally."

Dorothy immediately crossed her chest and headed straight for the kettle. "I'll make some tea."

Hannah returned her full attention to Liv. "Is Quentin with you?"

"He's here at the station. But not with me, with me. I think they've put him in a cell." Liv sounded on the verge of tears. "Oh, Hannah, after I've spoken to you, they're going to lock me up too."

Flashes of Liv hugging her knees in the corner of a dark dank, confined space flitted through Hannah's head. "Don't worry. It'll all get sorted. Once they realise whatever happened isn't your fault, they'll have no choice but to let you both go."

"But what if it doesn't get sorted? And we have to go to court? For something we didn't do?"

"Listen to me, Liv." Hannah spoke in a firm yet caring manner. "I promise you, that's not going to happen." Despite her calm exterior, Hannah's mind raced as she questioned what to do next. "Have you been charged with anything yet?"

"No. Apparently they're still investigating. But we could be here for up to twenty-four hours. You have to believe me, Hannah, we're innocent. We didn't do anything wrong."

"Of course, I believe you." Hannah was surprised her friend might think otherwise. "We just need to focus right now." *Think, think, think...* Hannah told herself. "Did the custody sergeant offer you any legal representation?"

"He said I was entitled to a solicitor when he read me my rights." Liv whimpered. "I can't believe I'm having to say that."

"Hold off on talking to a duty solicitor for now. I'll ring Carl."

"What can he do? He's in the South of France."

It was a fair enough question, but not only was Carl the best in the business, he was the only option Hannah could think of. She certainly couldn't sit around and do nothing when her friend needed help. "I don't know. But he'll think of something. Which police station are you at?"

"Leeds Central."

"Right. If the rally's still taking place, I'm guessing they'll be busy with that for now. Whatever investigations they talked about probably won't be done for a while. In the meantime, hold

SUZIE TULLETT

tight and don't say anything to the police until we've got you a proper advocate."

"I'm scared, Hannah."

Hannah paused for a second. The Liv she knew was loud and proud, a force to be reckoned with. Hearing her so frightened and out of her depth wasn't a Liv that Hannah recognised.

"I know. But you've no need to be." She took a deep breath. "I'm going to hang up now. Okay?" Hannah hated having to cut her friend off, but the quicker she did, the quicker they could get her out of there.

"Okay."

"I'll speak to you soon." Ending the call, Hannah immediately clicked to video call Carl. As she waited for him to pick up Dorothy placed a cup of tea in front of her. "Thank you," she said as the ringtone continued.

At last, the phone screen came to life and Carl appeared.

Hannah jumped to attention. "Finally."

Carl eyed her, suspicious. "To what do I owe this pleasure?"

"Pleasure is the last thing on my mind right now."

"That sounds ominous," Carl said.

"I need your help."

Carl smirked. "And I thought you'd rung to properly congratulate me on my new engagement."

"Congratulations, again," Hannah replied, her tone flat. "Now will you listen to me?"

Carl took a seat and gave Hannah his proper attention. "Go on."

"Liv's been arrested."

Carl suddenly appeared confused. "And the reason you're telling me this is?"

Hannah wasn't in the mood for games. "Because I want you to do something to help."

Carl let out a laugh. "In case you've forgotten, I'm not exactly in the office right now."

"Of course I haven't forgotten."

"Then what am I supposed to do? Carry out a client consultation via Zoom?" He continued to show his amusement. "I doubt any custody sergeant on the planet would go for that."

Hannah couldn't believe he found the whole thing funny. "This isn't something to joke about, Carl. A friend of mine is in trouble. Who happens to be innocent, by the way."

"Ha. That's what they all say."

Hannah didn't appreciate Carl's condescension at the best of times. "She was at some rally and got caught up in something. A wrong place, wrong time kind of thing."

Carl rolled his eyes, reiterating he'd heard it all before.

Seemingly getting nowhere, Hannah tried to appeal to his better nature. "Carl, I'm not asking you to fly back. But can't you at least give the police station a call? Talk to the custody sergeant on her behalf."

"And say what?"

"I don't know. You're the expert. It's not like you haven't dealt with cases like this before." Hannah scoffed. "Or is this below your pay scale these days?"

Carl smirked. "Actually, yes, if you–"

Hannah cut him off. "Don't be so arrogant." She recalled how she'd supported him at the beginning of his career. How he'd cut his teeth on cases just like Liv's. He might have gone on to represent the rich, famous, and probably downright guilty, but the foundations on which he built his career, were made from the Livs of the world.

Carl relented. "I'm sorry."

Hannah held her breath, anticipating what he'd say next.

"How about I ask a colleague to find out what's going on? Go in to speak to her if necessary? Which station is she at?"

At last, Hannah could relax. "Leeds Central." Hannah gave him a pointed look. "Not some trainee though."

Carl smiled at what he clearly saw as her cheek.

"I mean it, Carl. I want a proper lawyer involved. Someone who knows what they're doing."

Finally, the man relented. "Okay, okay. Let me see what I can do."

"Thank you. Oh, and her partner Quentin needs assistance too."

Carl's smile turned to a laugh. "You're not asking for much, are you." His finger hovered ready to end the call.

"Before you go," Hannah said.

Carl paused to listen.

"I really am pleased for you. For both of you."

Carl's expression softened. "I'll be in touch."

ollowing Liv's breaking news, Hannah's initial reaction had been to cancel that night's team bonding event. With her friend incarcerated in a police cell, Hannah certainly didn't have much of an appetite. But like Aunt Dorothy pointed out, Mel was looking forward to everyone meeting Russel, and Russel was probably already on a train and making his way up from the Midlands.

Of course, Hannah knew that left her feeling bad whether she cancelled or not, and in the end, she supposed she had no choice but to trust that Carl's colleague would come through and that Liv would be released as a matter of course.

With her hair straightened and pulled tight into a slick-look ponytail, Hannah checked out her reflection in her full-length floor mirror. She almost didn't recognise herself in the red and white floral brocade cocktail dress that Dorothy had insisted she buy. Of course, that meant getting shoes to go with it. Between them, they'd certainly shopped until they dropped following their lunch with Mel and Liv earlier that week.

Hannah twisted first one way and then the other, taking in the V-neckline that paralleled the V at the back. Its bodice was fitted, and its skirt flared showing off her streamlined waist perfectly. Hannah didn't know if she'd still be wearing the new ankle strapped heels come the end of the evening. But she was certainly starting it with style.

She thought back to when Beth had suggested Hannah wouldn't like the South of France because of its high-end glamour. "If you could see me now."

Reaching for her phone off the bedside table, Hannah's glee faded. Carl hadn't just kept his word; he'd surprised Hannah with a call-back to update her on what was happening. Carl had been at pains to reassure Hannah that his colleague was on it and Liv's arrest would come to nothing. But despite wanting to believe him, Hannah had yet to hear from Liv.

Hannah filled her cheeks with air and slowly exhaled. She told herself to stop worrying because for all she knew, Liv and Quentin could have already been released. At that very moment they could be racing home from the police station to change ready for the evening ahead. And by the time Hannah and Dorothy got to the restaurant, the two arrestees could be there waiting.

Refusing to be anything but positive, Hannah headed downstairs. She didn't have a clue how to properly walk in her heels and careful not to fall, she gripped the banister as she went. She paused in the kitchen doorway at the sight of Dorothy talking to Denis's urn.

"So what do you think?" Dorothy asked.

Hannah's heart melted. She was sure if he'd been there in person, Uncle Denis would have showered her aunt in compliments. Dorothy looked fabulous in her layered chiffon trouser suit. Its scoop neckline top with half-sleeves cascaded over a pair of wide-legged pants.

Dorothy began to twirl to show the urn her outfit from all angles, abruptly stopping halfway through when she clocked Hannah stood there watching.

"Don't we make a gorgeous pair," Hannah said with a big smile.

Dorothy put a hand to her chest as she looked back at Hannah. "We most certainly do." Her expression turned to one of concern. "Has Liv been in touch?"

Hannah shook her head. "Not yet."

"You know what they say; no news is good news."

Hannah hoped her aunt was right.

A car horn beeped, and Dorothy swung into action. "That'll be the taxi." She glanced around. "Now, where's my handbag?"

As she and Dorothy made their way outside, handbag found, Hannah locked the door behind them. She felt self-conscious as she tootled behind Dorothy and climbed into the car, forced to wonder if her shoes had been such a good idea after all. Having already twisted her ankle once and with a race to run the following week, the last thing Hannah needed was another injury.

"You'll be fine," Dorothy said, as if reading her mind.

The drive into town didn't take long and after paying the driver Hannah and Dorothy alighted the vehicle. Smoothing her dress down, Hannah suddenly felt nervous. Mel and Liv had never seen her so dressed up and the last thing she wanted was anyone thinking she'd made an effort for Gabe. A little voice questioned if subconsciously that might have been her intention. Another said, *so what if it was*. A third hoped Liv would be there to tease her regardless.

Dorothy nodded to the restaurant door. "Shall we?"

It was clear Dorothy was awestruck because she immediately admired the room's circular tables that were perfect for socialising. She oohed at the shiny silver cutlery and array of gleaming glasses sat on crisp white linen. And aahed at the space's rich wooden floor and the various ornate gold-framed pictures that adorned its matt black walls. "Very swish," Dorothy said.

While her aunt continued to be impressed, Hannah looked around for her friends. Spotting their table, there was no sign of Liv or Quentin, and Hannah's heart sank.

Dorothy squinted. "Mel's boyfriend's a bit older than I expected."

Hannah couldn't help but chuckle as she identified the man in question. "That's not Russel."

"Then who is it?"

"Gabe's dad."

Dorothy let out a laugh. "Thank goodness for that. I wouldn't have had a clue what to say if it *had* been."

The restaurant hostess stepped forward and led Hannah and Dorothy over to their seats.

As Gabe and Roger rose to their feet, Hannah couldn't help but feel impressed. Father and son had certainly gone to some effort. Roger looked great in his navy suit, and Gabe, wearing a crisp white shirt, grey fitted trousers, looked more gorgeous than ever.

As Gabe's eyes locked on Hannah, he seemed lost for words.

"Put your tongue back in, son," Roger said to Gabe, while Mel gave Hannah and Dorothy a hug.

"And you must be Dorothy," Roger said. "Lovely to meet you at last. I've heard so much about you."

As he moved to shake Dorothy's hand, she wavered as if not sure how to respond.

Hannah understood why. The way Dorothy continued to talk to Uncle Denis, she probably thought she was being disloyal.

"I believe you're the glue that's been holding this running team together," Roger said. Briefly glancing Hannah's way, he gave a discreet nod that said he understood Dorothy's hesitance. "I'd love to hear how you keep this one in line." Roger indicated Gabe. "In the nearly forty years since he was born, I've never quite managed it."

Dorothy relaxed and when Roger pulled a chair out for her to sit next to him, she willingly lowered herself into it. "I suppose we pensioners should stick together."

"Wine?" Roger asked, indicating a bottle of white that had sat in wait.

"Yes please," Dorothy said.

Roger proceeded to fill everyone's glasses.

"No Russel?" Hannah asked.

"Not yet. He has messaged. To say he's on his way. His train must be running late."

"And he knows to come straight here?" Gabe asked.

Mel took a deep breath in anticipation. She nodded.

Mel looked so nervous Hannah couldn't help but reach out and squeeze her friend's hand. Hannah checked her watch on her other wrist. "Has anyone heard from Liv or Quentin?"

"Nothing," Gabe said.

Mel shook her head. "Not a word."

"Fine team bonding session this is going to be with half the members missing," Dorothy said.

As Dorothy and Roger chatted amiably, Hannah, Mel and Gabe exchanged awkward glances. Not usually short of words, Hannah couldn't help but wonder if the stress of not knowing where Liv, Quentin and Russel were had weirded them out. "I hope the three of them are all right," Hannah said, having had enough of the silence. Glancing over at the door, it remained firmly shut. "Can you imagine if poor Russel's got lost. As for Liv and Quentin, they might not even have been released yet."

"Someone forgot to put on their positive pants," Gabe said.

Hannah laughed and glad someone had cut through the atmosphere, threw her napkin at him.

"Of course they're okay." Mel fidgeted in her seat, an action that belied her smile. "Although," she said, rising to her feet. "I might give Russel a quick ring. Just to make sure he's not sat in the wrong restaurant wondering where we are."

"Good idea," Hannah said.

Mel picked up her bag and headed outside.

"How are you getting on with the treadmill?" Gabe asked.

"Fine," Hannah replied. "I've been following your training plan."

"And is it helping?"

"I suppose I'll find out tomorrow. Although 2.5k in one go still feels unrealistic."

"If you need a cheerleader, remember I'm your man."

"Promise to wear spankies and wave pom-poms."

Gabe laughed. "I'll see what I can do."

"Sorry we're late, everyone."

Hannah looked up to see Liv standing there. Her eyes widened and she immediately jumped up from her seat to give Liv a big hug. "How're you feeling? What time did they let you go? Sit down. You've had one hell of a day."

"Tell that ex of yours we owe him a drink. Honestly, we can't thank him enough. Thanks to Carl's colleague and a city centre full of CCTV cameras, we were both released without charge."

"That's great news," Hannah said.

"No Slim?" Gabe asked, frowning.

"He's parking the car."

"I was beginning to think we'd have to start a campaign to free the cotton couple," Roger said, laughing. "I'm Roger. Gabe's dad."

"Pleased to meet you," Liv said, laughing. She glanced around, suddenly curious. "Where are Mel and Russel? I was looking forward to seeing them together."

"You mean you didn't see Mel on your way in?" Hannah asked. "She popped out to call him. She was worried he might have got lost."

"Well she's not out there now," Liv said.

The restaurant door swung open, and a handsome gentleman walked in.

Liv preened. "Here he is, my Quentin."

Gabe shook his head. "I don't think I'll ever get used to hearing him called that."

Hannah took in the blond haired, green-eyed hunk of a man, as he approached. "Pleased to meet you, at last," Hannah said. From his appearance alone she could see why Liv was attracted to him. He had the most fantastic cheekbones and a well-groomed beard, and tall wasn't the word. He towered above Liv.

"You too," he replied.

"Ooh, Liv, he's gorgeous," Dorothy said. Shaking his hand, she was slow to let go. She turned to Gabe. "I'm sorry to say this, but you have some strong competition for my affections right now."

Gabe clutched his chest. "I'm wounded."

"Did you see anyone on your way in?" Liv asked Quentin.

He shook his head. "Not a soul."

"It's just that Mel's gone AWOL."

"I hope she's all right," Dorothy said.

Gabe got up from his seat. "I'll go and have a scout about, shall I?"

Hannah nodded and Gabe made his way outside. Reappearing, he shrugged.

"Where could she have gone?" Dorothy asked.

Hannah sighed as she silently cursed the ground Russel walked on. "I think she's gone home."

CHAPTER 38

*H*annah stared at the running machine, plucking up the courage to get started. She'd come so far in her running journey, the last thing she wanted to do was fail. Completing the 2.5k had felt daunting enough, but to try doing it after hardly any sleep seemed like madness.

Hannah had lain awake until the early hours worrying about Mel. It wasn't like her to disappear like that. Hannah could still feel the panic as she and Liv kept trying and failing to contact their vanishing friend. Hannah ended up leaving a voicemail threatening to go round with Liv and bang on the door until Mel let them in. Which finally and thankfully elicited a response.

Mel simply needed a bit of space to think. She insisted they both had no reason to worry, and they were to continue enjoying their evening. Yes, it was good to know she wasn't dead in a ditch somewhere or kidnapped. As for having a nice evening, that was something easier said than done.

Pulling herself together, Hannah refused to use Mel's distress as an excuse to get out of that day's running challenge. She had to get on with it no matter how tired she felt. Hannah knew if she didn't, all the work she'd put in those last weeks would be for nothing. And boy had she worked.

Thanks to Gabe's training schedule, the previous training days had been particularly challenging. Following each initial five-minute warm-up walk, Hannah had run for longer periods than she'd been used to.

Taking a deep breath, she couldn't believe she was about to try jogging non-stop for 2.5k. And not only that, in thirty minutes or under. Hannah sighed, deciding that whoever had come up with the one-hour cut-off point in which to complete the whole race, mustn't be very nice.

Unable to delay it any longer, Hannah began the session with her usual tricep stretches and side lunges. Putting her hands flat against the wall, she threw in a few calf exercises for good measure. After jiggling her whole body to properly loosen up, she stepped onto the conveyor belt and tapped the relevant LCD icons.

As the treadmill sprang to life and Hannah started yet another warm-up walk, she covered her ears with her headphones. If her playlist didn't keep her moving for the whole 2.5k, then nothing would.

At last, setting off on a jog, Hannah's steps followed the beat of the music. Making sure to breathe in through her nose and out through her mouth, she felt comfortable at the pace she'd set herself. With her head up and chest forward, she kept her gaze away from the timer. Hannah knew from experience that when things got tough, the countdown seemed to take forever.

After a while, Hannah could feel the effects of her running. Her heart rate sped up, small sweat patches formed on her T-shirt, and there was a burn in her calves. "You can do this," she said, refusing to acknowledge her inner voice that suggested it was time to give up.

Determined to keep going, Hannah geed herself on by thinking back to her first running attempt. On that occasion, she'd only got to the end of her street when she needed to slow into a walk. Hannah couldn't believe how completely breathless she'd been, let alone how much her heart had pounded. Then again, she'd supposed it understandable. Most of her life was spent on her bum.

It didn't matter how much running around Hannah did for Beth and Archie, Hannah had to admit most of it was done from the driver's seat of her car. Going up and down stairs with the laundry and pushing a trolley around the supermarket might up Hannah's step count, but any benefit was quickly offset with the amount of time she sat behind her desk at work. She knew that day's 2.5k challenge might not seem a lot to most people, but Hannah felt proud. It was testament to how far she'd come.

Hannah caught sight of Aunt Dorothy who popped her head into the room. "Fifteen minutes in," she said, raising her voice to be heard over Hannah's headphones. "You're already at the halfway point." Dorothy gave Hannah a big smile and put her thumbs up as a sign of encouragement. "You've got this."

A hand waving a pom-pom suddenly appeared behind Dorothy's head and remembering her conversation with Gabe the previous evening, Hannah knew it could only belong to him. She laughed as Gabe finally revealed himself. Stepping into the room to wave two pom-poms, Hannah had an idea he'd probably gone out and bought them especially.

"You're doing great," he said.

"Thank you," Hannah said, shouting above the music, before Dorothy and Gabe turned around and left her to it.

Hannah kept going despite feeling increasingly uncomfortable. As her breathing began to labour, it would have been easy to stop, but she knew she would only be letting herself and the team down if she did. Apart from during pregnancy and childbirth, Hannah had never physically stretched herself to that degree and she wasn't going to let one racing pulse and two chaffing thighs prevent her from reaching her goal.

She'd experienced various challenges over the years, of course. Learning how to care for two babies at once had been testing. As had overcoming the countless worries, stresses and strains that came with being a single mum. But the sponsored race was the first personal challenge since her university days that involved Hannah and Hannah alone. Once she fell pregnant, life became about everyone else.

Thinking about it, it was as if the sponsored run represented something bigger. Like the start of a new beginning, Hannah considered. It felt like a springboard from which Hannah could catapult herself into a different way of doing things; an opportunity that both excited and scared her.

Ever since she'd signed up to the race, the signs that something needed to change had been there. Such as the fact that without her children, Hannah was lost. She might not have liked her mum's comment about it not being long before Beth and Archie were off to university, but it had been a stark eye-opener. Then there was Dorothy. Her loneliness had been like a glimpse into Hannah's future if things remained as they were. Even Hannah's own children had put their foot down and cut her hours.

"In through the nose, out through the mouth," Hannah told herself.

As frightening as it felt, Hannah couldn't deny it was time to embrace a new future and although not quite there, if she could go from zero to 5k and see the race through in a total of four weeks, surely she could cope with a few changes.

The treadmill's LCD screen beeped and seeing the timer start to flash, at last, Hannah's thirty minutes were up. She slowed to a walk, almost tearful to note that she hadn't only lasted timewise, at just over 2.5 kilometres, she'd more than gone the distance.

Hannah whipped off her headphones. "Aunt Dorothy, Gabe! I've only gone and thrashed it!"

Sodding her cool-down walk, as the two of them entered the

room Hannah immediately stopped the treadmill and jumped off the conveyor belt. Whipping off her headphones, she hastened to give first Dorothy and then Gabe a hug. "I hope you both know I couldn't have done it without you."

"You certainly could," Dorothy said, having none of it. Her expression relaxed. "Oh, Hannah, I'm so proud of you." She came over all excited. "Just think, this time next week you'll have done 5k."

"Well done, Hannah," Gabe said.

Surprising Hannah, he pulled her close and squeezing her, kissed the top of her head. Even more surprising was the fact that she didn't pull away. Enjoying the moment, she leant her head against his chest and breathing in his scent, wrapped her arms around him in return.

CHAPTER 39

ONE WEEK UNTIL RACE DAY

With Aunt Dorothy in the passenger seat, Hannah pulled over to the kerb and switched off her car engine. She glanced around trying to spot Liv. "Looks like I'm the first to arrive for once." Hannah reached for her phone. "I'm even on time." She showed Dorothy the clock on her phone screen.

"That's because you're a good friend. Someone to count on in an emergency." Dorothy cradled the casserole dish she had balanced on her lap. "Liv won't be far behind."

Hannah scrolled through her mobile to read Liv's text again. Liv had messaged to say that like Hannah, she was worried about Mel. Not only had Mel continued with her radio silence, she'd also failed to turn up for work that day. Something that really got the alarm bells ringing. Mel never took time off. Leaving them no choice but to pay her a visit whether she wanted one or not.

Hannah clocked a car slowing to a standstill in her rear-view mirror and immediately recognised it as Liv's. "She's here," Hannah said, stuffing her phone away, before she and Dorothy climbed out.

Alighting her vehicle, Liv held up a carrier bag. "I've brought chocolates."

"Good call," Hannah replied.

"And I've brought a stew," Dorothy said, indicating her offering.

Hannah took a deep breath. "Are we all ready?"

Dorothy and Liv nodded, before following Hannah to Mel's front door.

Liv rapped hard on the glass.

When Mel didn't answer, Hannah moved to the lounge window and peered in. "I can't see her…" She placed her ear against the glass. "But she's definitely in. I can hear music." She turned to the others. "Sad music."

Liv crouched down and looked through the letter box. "We're not going anywhere, Mel!" she shouted through. "So you may as well let us in."

With no response Liv rose to her feet again. "What now?"

"It would seem we're here for the long haul," Hannah said.

Dorothy gave a definite nod. "I agree."

After a few moments, Hannah heard a key turn in the latch. "At last."

The door slowly opened to reveal a sorry-looking Mel.

Hannah immediately gave her friend a sympathetic smile and stepping forward, wrapped Mel in a huge bear hug. "You poor thing."

Hannah, at last, let go. Taking in Mel's appearance, it seemed she and Liv were right to be worried. Mel's eyes weren't just red, they appeared sore. Her nostrils were peeling and her hair clearly hadn't seen a brush or a squirt of shampoo for days. A fresh pair of pyjamas wouldn't have gone amiss either.

Without saying a word, Mel turned and traipsed into the lounge, leaving Hannah, Dorothy and Liv to let themselves in.

"It's worse than I imagined," Dorothy said, closing the door behind them.

"I thought these might cheer you up." Liv produced the chocolates from the carrier bag and handed them over.

Mel seemed on automatic pilot as she sat on the sofa, opened them, and stuffed one into her mouth. "Apparently Russel's train broke down." She let out a hollow laugh. "Likely story." She sighed. "I bet it wasn't even him in that picture. It'll be of some random dude whose photo he nicked off the internet." She ate another chocolate. "How could I have been so stupid?"

Hannah sat down next to her. "You're nothing of the sort."

Liv took the seat on Mel's other side, while Dorothy sat in a chair.

"I won't have you talking about yourself like that," Liv said.

"Why not?" Mel stuffed yet another chocolate into her mouth.

"Because it's not true," Dorothy replied.

"I really wanted to believe him about the video call. You know. When he said his camera was broken. But I knew deep down he was lying."

"He might not have been," Hannah said, trying to sound hopeful.

"Now *you're* treating me like I'm stupid." Mel ate another chocolate.

That had been far from Hannah's intention. The last thing she wanted was to make Mel feel worse. "Have you had a proper meal today?"

Mel shook her head.

"Did you eat yesterday?" Liv asked.

Again, Mel shook her head.

Dorothy rose to her feet. "Leave it with me." Taking her casserole dish with her, she headed off in search of the kitchen.

"Liv, do you fancy running our friend here a bath?" Hannah asked.

Liv stood. "With pleasure."

As Liv exited the room, Hannah took the box of chocolates from Mel and put it to one side. She sat in silence, waiting for her friend to speak.

"He keeps messaging," Mel finally said. "Begging me to tell

him what he's done to upset me." A sob escaped her mouth as she took a deep breath and exhaled. "You'll be pleased to know I haven't answered. I've wasted enough time on that man." Falling quiet again, another sob escaped Mel's lips, but she gathered herself. "You and Liv probably think I was naïve and foolish for trusting him in the first place."

"We thought no such thing."

"But you didn't read the things he said to me. You didn't see how he made me laugh. He's got a way with words that makes you feel special. And I know we'd never met, but…"

"You developed feelings for him?"

Mel nodded. "Ridiculous, hey?" Fat globules of silent tears suddenly ran down her cheeks.

Hannah understood Mel's heartbreak. Hannah didn't think she'd ever forget the pain she'd experienced when she found out Carl wasn't the man she'd thought he was. The anguish had coursed through her veins and seared in her chest. Back then Hannah couldn't eat or sleep. Neither did she have the energy or inclination to look after herself.

At times, Hannah thought she'd die her heart was so broken. But she hadn't had the luxury of giving up all together. She had to keep going for Beth and Archie's sake until gradually the agony began to lessen. "It gets easier," Hannah said. "I promise."

Mel's bottom lip quivered. "I wish I could believe you." She began to properly cry.

Hannah pulled Mel close and hugging her, let her bawl her eyes out.

"Bath's ready," Liv said. Entering the room, she fell silent at the sight of Mel's sorrow.

Mel straightened up and wiping her eyes with her sleeve, pulled herself together. She looked from Liv to Hannah. "Thank you for coming. I think I really need a friend or two right now."

"Make that three," Dorothy said, giving Mel a warm compassionate smile as she appeared in the doorway.

CHAPTER 40

*A*fter Monday evening's visit to see Mel, Hannah's focus on her training had never been better. Such was her anger toward Russel, she'd thrashed every session she'd done on the treadmill. It was as if every step was an *up yours* to the man. Hannah scoffed. Every cloud and all that.

As she finished that day's cool-down walk, Hannah still couldn't rid herself of Mel's pain. She'd never understood how one human being could knowingly hurt another like that. Mel was such a kind-hearted individual. She deserved so much better.

"And you want me to start dating again?" Hannah said, of Beth and Archie.

Hannah couldn't believe she'd begun to consider the fact that her children might be right. After seeing Mel's distress, Hannah thought it no wonder she'd questioned their limited wisdom and was leaning towards staying single, after all. While at Mel's house, not only had Hannah felt her friend's pain at the hands of Russel, she'd relived some of the hurt she, herself, had experienced thanks to Carl.

Hannah took off her headphones and wiped her forehead down with the edge of her T-shirt. Desperate for a glass of water, she made her way through to the kitchen. "Gabe," she said, surprised to see him sat at the table with Aunt Dorothy. "What are you doing here?"

"I had a break between clients, so I dropped in to see how the training's going."

"And to deliver an invitation," Dorothy said.

Hannah's eyes widened in interest.

"Roger has invited me over for dinner." Dorothy waved a piece of paper. "He's written down his address and apparently isn't taking no for an answer."

Hannah headed over to a cupboard. "Very nice." Taking out a glass, she turned on the cold tap and filled it with water.

"He wants to cook me his Risotto alla Milanese, which–"

"According to legend," Hannah jumped in. "Was invented by the workmen building the Milan Cathedral."

"Was it?" Dorothy asked in amazement.

Hannah nodded, while Gabe seemed impressed.

"*I* was going to say it's one of Roger's specialities. Your point is far more interesting."

"Apparently, they were using saffron to dye the stained-glass windows." Hannah drank a mouthful of water. "And figured they'd also throw it into their rice."

"Weren't they worried it might make them sick?" Dorothy asked.

"Obviously not," Hannah replied.

"I'm surprised I got an invite at all. I'd have thought Roger considered us all barmy. What with Liv's arrest, Mel disappearing, and you, Hannah, spending most of the night like you had the world on your shoulders. Don't get me wrong. I understand you were worried about Mel. But it wasn't quite the team-building exercise we'd hoped for, eh."

"How is Mel?" Gabe asked.

Meeting his gaze, Hannah sighed. "She'll get there." Forcing herself to look away, she turned her attention to her aunt. "So, when is this dinner of yours?"

"Tonight."

"That's a bit short notice."

"Dad can be a bit spontaneous, shall we say." Gabe opened his mouth to add something else but changed his mind.

"What?" Hannah asked. Waiting for him to speak, Gabe appeared nervous. It was a side of him that Hannah hadn't seen before.

"I was just thinking, while they're enjoying dinner, maybe we could grab that coffee we talked about." He coughed as if clearing his throat a little. "If you're up for it?"

Hannah hesitated. The way she was feeling thanks to Russel, she doubted she'd be very good company.

"To talk tactics, of course," Gabe added. "The race is only a few days off."

Hannah opened her mouth to explain, but Dorothy got in there first.

"What a brilliant idea. As team leader, I don't know why I didn't think of that." She gave Hannah an adamant look, making it clear the matter wasn't up for discussion.

"Great," Gabe said. He rose to his feet ready to leave. "See you both at mine then. Around seven o'clock?"

"Seven's fine," Dorothy said. "Isn't it, Hannah?"

With no choice but to agree, Hannah willed Gabe to leave so she could ask her aunt what she was playing at.

It seemed Hannah wasn't the only one waiting to speak. As soon as the front door opened then closed, Dorothy jumped in before Hannah got the chance. "I know what you're thinking. That I shouldn't have bulldozed you into going for a drink just then."

"No, Aunt Dorothy, you shouldn't."

"Would it help if I told you I did it for both our sakes?"

Hannah didn't follow.

191

Dorothy sighed and patted the chair next to her, encouraging Hannah to sit down.

Rolling her eyes, Hannah did as requested.

"When it comes to these social-type situations, we're both the same, you and me."

Hannah didn't see how.

"We're afraid," Dorothy said. "I'm scared that having dinner with another man means I'm being disloyal to Denis. Of course my head knows it's only a plate of risotto. And that Roger is just being kind. I mean, as a widow, he understands how hard it is being the one left behind. Then there's my heart." Dorothy looked over at Denis's urn. "Which thinks I'm betraying the only man I've ever loved."

Hannah reached out to her aunt with a comforting hand.

"And now we come to you."

Throwing herself back in her seat, Hannah sighed. "I thought we might."

"You're scared because of what Carl did. And while your head insists that not all men are the same, your heart is telling you it doesn't want to get broken again."

Hannah opened her mouth to respond but quickly realised her aunt hadn't finished.

"There's no point denying it. I saw your reaction to Mel's pain the other night. It obviously opened old wounds for you. But you can't let past experiences, or what Mel's going through, prevent you from getting what you deserve."

"And what's that?"

"Real happiness."

Hannah wanted nothing more. She just wasn't sure a relationship would provide it.

"Now we both know I'd be beyond delighted if you and Gabe got to know each other better."

Hannah let out a laugh. "You don't say."

"But whether it's with him, or someone you haven't yet met,

you shouldn't deny yourself the opportunity of finding someone who loves you more than he loves himself."

"Is that what you had with Denis."

A sadness seemed to wash over Dorothy. "I certainly did."

Just the thought of getting that deep into a relationship filled Hannah with dread.

"Which brings me full circle. We both have to force ourselves into the situations we fear most."

"What's your biggest fear?" Hannah asked.

"Feeling lonely again. So, when I go home to Norfolk, I need to get out there instead of shutting myself away." Dorothy smiled. "In the short time I've been here, thanks to you and Mel and Liv, I've learnt that I don't need to be in a couple to make new friends. I don't have to sit at home talking to four walls if I don't want to. I can build the semblance of a life without Denis."

"Of course you can."

"And you, young lady, must open your heart to at least the possibility of finding love." Dorothy fell pensive for a moment. "That's what I admire most about Mel. She knew people would judge if she built a meaningful relationship with a chap she'd never even seen, never mind met. But she'd taken that risk anyway. And who can say, it might still pay off."

Hannah scoffed, doubting that very much.

"And look at Liv. She's considering travelling to Africa to build schools from the ground up with a man she hasn't known for two minutes. How's that for a leap into the unknown?" Dorothy reached up and put her hand against Hannah's cheek. "I want *you* to have adventures of the heart like Mel and Liv, Hannah. I know it's scary, but from one who knows, find the right man and it's worth it." She let her hand drop. "But like I said, you have to force yourself."

Hannah filled her cheeks with air and exhaled, not sure she could do it.

CHAPTER 41

*H*annah was impressed as she tried to identify Gabe's house. With a green open space on one side of the road and a row of little cottages on the other, his street was a hidden gem that sat on the edge of town. One that she hadn't even known existed. "What number does it say?" she asked as she continued to admire the rose gardened properties.

Aunt Dorothy glanced at the sheet of paper. "Number 7."

Hannah slowed, so her aunt could check out the digits on each door.

Dorothy squinted. "This is it," she suddenly said.

Pulling over, Hannah took in the windy stone paved pathway that led to a cute little front door. She couldn't help but picture Gabe having to duck every time he entered and exited. Ivy climbed around the windows, under which sat pots of colourful flowers. Everything she saw was a complete surprise. She'd had Gabe down as a centre of town loft apartment kind of guy.

As Hannah and Dorothy got out of the car and approached the house, Gabe appeared at the cottage door. He wore faded jeans, a white T-shirt and a navy shirt he'd left unbuttoned. His hair was wet as if he'd not long stepped out of the shower. Seeing him, Hannah's chest suddenly felt light, and she took a deep breath hoping it would settle the fluttering in her tummy.

"Please," Gabe said. "Come in." Stepping to one side, he welcomed Hannah and Dorothy into his home. "Dad's in the kitchen." Leading the way, Gabe lowered his head to avoid it hitting the beams.

Hannah glanced around as she went. A pale blue throw covered the arm of a comfy-looking cream sofa, in front of which sat a simple glass coffee table. A pale yellow checked armchair sat by the hearth, home to an open fire. A floral rug partially covered the bare floorboards. To say two men lived there, the cottage felt like it wasn't short of a woman's touch.

The kitchen was just as sweet, Hannah considered. With its wooden beams, three white-washed walls, and one of exposed stonework, it had a Belfast sink and traditional solid fuel range. Thanks to its navy-blue units and white granite worktops the room was a perfect mix of old and new. But just like the lounge, it had a feminine feel.

"This is lovely," Dorothy said, glancing around. "And something does smell good."

Roger beamed. "I hope you're hungry, because if not you're taking home a doggy bag."

"Starving," Dorothy replied. "I've been saving myself all day."

"Shall we leave them to it?" Gabe asked.

Hannah looked to Dorothy. The last thing she wanted was to leave her aunt in a strange house if she wasn't properly comfortable.

Dorothy discreetly nodded, indicating that all was well.

"You've got my number," Hannah said. Not that she got a response. Before Hannah and Gabe had got to the front door Dorothy and Roger were chatting like old friends. Expecting to jump back in her car, Hannah fumbled in her pocket for her keys.

"You don't need those," Gabe said, as they stepped outside.

"There's a place around the corner that does a great range in coffees."

Tucking the keys away again, Hannah breathed in the fresh air as she observed the park users. Families played cricket, dogs chased balls, and young couples sat on blankets chatting. At 7pm it was still early, and Hannah couldn't blame them for making the most of the evening sun.

Hannah's arm brushed against Gabe's as they strolled side by side, causing Hannah's nerves to tingle. Scolding herself, she insisted they were simply going for a coffee to talk running tactics. They were in no way out on a date.

Acknowledging the silence between them, Hannah tried to think of something to say. She and Gabe didn't usually struggle to converse and the longer the quiet went on, the more self-conscious Hannah felt.

"Here we are," Gabe said, as they turned the corner. "In or out?"

Hannah glanced over at the traditional pub and thanks to its small and, no doubt, deep-sill original windows, didn't fancy sitting in a darkened room. She much preferred the wooden picnic tables that sat on the gravelled patio. "Out," Hannah said. "It'd be a shame to miss the last of the sunshine."

While Hannah sat down, Gabe headed inside, and glancing around, Hannah continued to feel awkward. Love-struck couples held hands across their tables. Others were sat next to each other so they could share in-jokes and whisper sweet nothings. Women played with their hair as their partners gazed into their eyes.

A part of Hannah felt jealous. She liked the idea of Gabe stroking her hand with his thumb as they chatted. Telling herself she was being silly, she again reminded herself of the fact that unlike her fellow customers, she wasn't having an assignation.

Gabe reappeared with a tray containing what looked like two soup mugs but, as he grew closer, Hannah could see contained coffee.

She let out a laugh at the amount of caffeine she was about to consume. "I'm obviously not going to sleep tonight."

"I'd be happy to keep you company."

Choosing not to answer, Hannah blushed. She liked the idea of that too.

"So, how's the training going?"

"Good," Hannah replied, glad to be on safer ground. "The plan you gave me is brilliant. It's done wonders for my stamina and confidence."

"Then my job is done."

Watching him break open a little packet of sugar cubes and pop one into his cup, Hannah took in his easy demeanour. She considered the fact that she probably wouldn't see Gabe again after that week and his smile was one of the things she'd miss.

"I know I shouldn't," Gabe said. He dropped another sugar lump into his drink and stirred. "But I can't drink coffee without it."

As Hannah picked up her cup and drank, a little voice told her his smile wasn't the only thing she'd miss. Hannah took a deep breath, daring to admit the little voice was right.

Gabe looked up. "What?"

Hannah hadn't realised she was staring. "Tell me about yourself."

"Why?"

"Because I'm interested."

Gabe finally put his teaspoon down. "There's not a lot to tell."

"Come on. You know all about my boring life. That I'm divorced with two children, and I have a crap job. That I'm about to take part in a charity race that I might not finish, and that I have an aunt from Norfolk. *And* you know I have a batty mother."

Gabe clearly struggled to keep a straight face. "Janice, yes. How can I forget?"

"You've met Mel and Liv, the bestest friends any woman could have. You've even said hello to my ex-husband and children."

"Ah, but I don't know the things that matter."

Hannah looked back at him, perplexed. "Such as?"

"Your favourite colour."

Hannah liked the fact that he thought the little things were important. "Green."

"Favourite number?"

"Four."

"Favourite food?"

"Too many to mention."

Gabe laughed.

"All I know about you is that you're a personal trainer, friends with Quentin and that you're Roger's son. Oh, and as of this evening, that you live in a quaint little cottage."

"To be honest, that pretty much sums everything up."

Hannah didn't believe that for one second. "Why do you live in a cottage, by the way? Why not some bachelor pad with a gaming chair and a console."

Gabe laughed. "Is that how you see me?"

"That's my point. I've only got my imagination to go off."

Gabe flashed her a look. "Tell me more."

Hannah eyes widened. "Not that kind of imagination." She took another sip of coffee. "I do know one other thing about you."

"And what's that?"

"You're very good at deflection."

"What do you mean?"

"See, you did it again." Hannah laughed. "Every time I ask a question, you answer it with one of your own."

"Maybe I'm trying to create an air of mystery. I thought you women like that?"

Hannah shook her head. "And there it is again."

"I'm sorry. I'm just not used to talking about myself." He drank some coffee. "Okay, here goes. I've been a full-time personal trainer for just over two years. Before that I worked in IT."

"Really?" Hannah's eyes widened. "That is a surprise. Seeing you as a gamer is one thing. I'd never have had you down as an outright computer techie."

"Why not?"

"Because IT workers don't usually look like Greek gods." As soon as her words were out, Hannah regretted them.

"And I do, do I?" Gabe held her gaze a tad longer than necessary and feeling her cheeks redden Hannah was forced to look away.

"Why the switch?" she asked, composing herself.

"When Mum died it was obvious Dad wasn't coping very well."

Hannah understood why. Aunt Dorothy had struggled after Uncle Denis's death.

"When he moved in with me, I wanted to be able to work my own hours. I'd always been a fitness freak, and personal training seemed a natural choice." Gabe picked up his cup. "I have no children." He took a couple of gulps. "Neither do I have any siblings."

"Why are you still single?"

Gabe stared at Hannah. "Registering your interest, are you?"

"And if I was?" With yet more unwanted words spilling out of her mouth, Hannah wondered what was wrong with her.

"Now who's deflecting." As Gabe glanced over Hannah's shoulder, his expression froze.

Curious as to why, Hannah turned to see a woman walking in their direction. No wonder she'd caught his eye; the woman was stunning.

She had long, dark shiny hair that spilled down her shoulders, gorgeous brown eyes, and full plump lips. Like Hannah, the woman wore hardly any make-up. However, whereas Hannah abstained because she couldn't do with the fuss, the woman before her simply didn't need it. Neither did she need to dress up. Teamed with a plain black fitted T-shirt, the woman's black skinny jeans and bright red high heels weren't just simple, they emphasised her already-long legs. Much to her surprise, the woman approached their table.

"Roger told me you'd probably be here, Gabe," the woman said.

Hannah looked to Gabe, who for some reason appeared furious. "What's going on?" Hannah asked. "Who is this?" When Gabe didn't answer, Hannah redirected her attention to the woman. "Who are you?"

"I think that's a question *I* should be asking?" The woman held out her hand for Hannah to shake. "I'm Kate."

Recalling that same name come up on Gabe's phone, Hannah's confusion grew. She couldn't understand why a client of Gabe's would unexpectedly turn up like that. Gingerly accepting the gesture, Kate's grip felt firmer than Hannah thought necessary.

Kate smirked. "Do you want to tell her, or shall I?"

Gabe's eyes pleaded with Kate not to.

"Gabe?" Hannah said.

Still, he stayed quiet.

"All right then," Kate said, clearly enjoying herself. "If you won't, I will." She happily gave Hannah her full attention. "I'm Gabe's wife."

CHAPTER 42

"*H*annah!" Desperate, Gabe willed her to come back. Gabe's threw his arms upwards as he watched her march into the distance without a second glance. He ran his hands through his hair, frustrated that she hadn't given him the opportunity to explain. He stepped forward ready to go after her, but as she disappeared round the corner, he realised there was no point. Hannah had already made it clear she thought Gabe secretive. The fact that he hadn't told her he had a wife proved her observation correct. He spun round to face Kate and glared at her. "What do you want?"

"Did I interrupt something?"

Knowing some people never changed, Gabe could see Kate was getting off on the fact that she had. He continued to glower. Having not seen her for two years, he couldn't believe she had the audacity to turn up without warning.

Kate sneered as she glanced in the direction Hannah had taken. "I wouldn't have had her down as your type."

"What's that supposed to mean?" Gabe felt his hackles rise further. Whatever the reason for Kate's visit, it had nothing to do with Hannah. Kate could keep her out of it.

"She's a bit plain, don't you think?"

Gabe knew Kate was baiting him, trying to ascertain how much he cared about Hannah. Oh, the fun she could have with that information. But Gabe refused to bite and instead calmed himself. Kate could say what she'd come to say then leave.

Kate shrugged. "Each to their own, I suppose." She took a seat at the picnic table, letting Gabe know that events would follow her timetable, not his. "Aren't you going to buy me a drink?"

"Why would I do that?"

"I don't know." Kate smirked. "For old times' sake?"

Gabe scoffed. As far as he was concerned, nothing about their past life together was worth celebrating.

"I take it you got my letter," she said.

"Is that why you're here?"

"I tried phoning too, but you will ignore my calls." Kate made a show of admiring her fingernails.

"You could have left a message."

"Before or after you blocked my number? Let's face it, you didn't give me any choice *but* to come and see you." She paused. "Interesting." She let her hand drop and gave Gabe a mocking look. "Maybe that was your plan all along? Maybe you still want me back?"

"Are you done?" Gabe asked. Because he was.

"All you had to do was open the envelope."

When Kate first left, Gabe had lived in the hope that she might come back. Saying she needed some space, Gabe did everything in his power to try to make things right. He'd attempted to talk through their issues and when that didn't work, he'd responded to her every whim. Whatever Kate wanted Kate got.

Of course she'd hint that there was a chance they could make things work, and such was Gabe's love for her, he couldn't see what everyone else saw. That she was playing him for all she could get. Gabe scoffed. Finding her with another man was the real icing on the cake. Up until then, she made him believe their relationship still had a future.

For a long time, the gut-wrenching pain of Kate's infidelity would creep up, forcing Gabe to live the experience all over again. He tried to move on, but it took a long time for him to get over it. At one point, he wasn't sure he ever would. Finally, his anguish began to fade, until one day he felt nothing.

Then out of the blue he met Hannah, with her ugly crying and her what you see is what you get attitude. She made him laugh without even trying and plucked obscure facts out of nowhere. For all her weirdness, Hannah had awakened the possibility of there being a real life after Kate. She made him feel things he never thought he'd feel again.

"Like I said. What do you want?"

Kate laughed. "Who says I want anything?"

Gabe shook his head and moved to leave. Kate was always after something, a lesson he learned a long time ago.

"I want a divorce," Kate said.

CHAPTER 43

*H*annah was dripping in sweat. She'd known it was too hot for an outdoor run when she'd set out, but she'd been going stir-crazy and needed to channel her frustrations somehow. If Russel's behaviour had fired her up, that was nothing to what Gabe's had done.

Relieved to be almost home, the sun beat down on her back. She felt the strain of her feet pounding on the pavement, each step hurting more than the last. Her throat was dry from not concentrating on her breathing and whereas running usually gave her the space to think, her mind refused to settle. The scene with Gabe and Kate constantly played on a loop and no matter how hard she tried, she couldn't get her head around it.

She came to a standstill and let herself into the house. Passing the lounge on her way to the kitchen, Hannah paused, scowling as she glanced into the room. She knew she was making life hard for herself and, no doubt, being childish, but having discovered Gabe was married, she no longer wanted anything to do with the man and that included using his treadmill.

She heard Aunt Dorothy chatting and after assuming she was talking to Uncle Denis, the room fell quiet when Hannah entered.

Wondering why, she was surprised to see Mel and Liv sat at the dining table. "No one told me we were having a team meeting," Hannah said. She headed straight for the sink to get a glass of water. "Although with only two days until race day I suppose it makes sense."

"Sod the race," Liv said. "When you didn't turn up for last night's group training session, we wanted to check you're okay."

Hannah took a long hard drink to both quench her thirst and soothe her sore throat. She wiped her mouth with the back of her hand and turned to face the others. "Why wouldn't I be?"

"Poor Gabe was beside himself," Mel said.

"Tell that to someone who cares," Hannah replied.

Dorothy, Liv and Mel shared a knowing look. "Didn't I tell you she's in denial?"

"If this is about Gabe's marital status," Hannah said. "You're all worrying over nothing. Was I surprised to find out he has a wife? Yes. Is that any of my business? No."

"You're really trying to tell us you don't care?" Liv asked.

Hannah joined them at the table. "That's exactly what I'm telling you." Her phone rang in her pocket and realising its timing could have been better, Hannah fixed a smile on her face.

Dorothy, Mel and Liv stared back at her. They clearly knew as much as Hannah did that it was probably Gabe trying to get through and while Hannah's expression masked the fact that inside she was squirming, theirs dared her to pick up.

Much to Hannah's relief, her phone, at last, fell silent. "As I was saying, the man means nothing to me."

Dorothy raised an eyebrow. "If that's the case, why won't you talk to him?"

"That's a fair enough question," Liv said.

"I'm sure you can spare Gabe five minutes," Mel said. "Not only has he given up his time for you these last couple of weeks, we're all–"

"You're gonna play the guilt card now?"

Mel ignored Hannah's question. "As I was about to say, we're all mature enough to know things aren't always what we think they are."

Hannah scoffed. If anyone should understand her position, she'd have thought it was Mel. "Spoken to Russel lately, have you?"

Mel immediately appeared hurt.

"Hannah!" Dorothy and Liv said.

Realising she'd crossed a line, Hannah's upper body crumpled. Gabe's marital status wasn't Mel's fault and Hannah had no right to take it out on her friend. Full of regret, she closed her eyes for a second. "I'm sorry," she said, before opening them again. "That was uncalled for. Please. I didn't mean it."

"I suppose I did walk into that," Mel said.

"No, you didn't." Hannah took a deep breath and exhaled. "I know it's no excuse, but I'm just tired. I've been preparing for Saturday's race and–"

"You've been using it as a distraction, you mean," Dorothy interrupted. "And running yourself into the ground in the process." She turned to Mel and Liv. "I've tried to tell her. She's been pushing herself far too much. Gabe's training plan has gone out of the window. It's like she's trying to prove something, although I haven't a clue what."

"Can we please stop talking about Gabe?" Hannah asked, surprising even herself with how loud she'd spoken.

Dorothy, Mel and Liv stared at Hannah, shocked.

"Okay then," Dorothy said. "Putting on my team leader hat for a minute, I'm worried you're not going to get to the end." She gave Hannah a knowing look. "Don't think I haven't noticed your limp's back."

"Hannah, why would you risk injuring yourself again?" Mel sighed. "I bet you haven't focused on your breathing either, have you?"

Hannah let out a laugh. "You and your bloody breathing."

"It's not funny," Liv said. "The last thing we want is you getting hurt."

It's a bit late for that, Hannah thought but didn't say.

"And neither has she taken any rest days," Dorothy said. "Don't think you're running tomorrow, young lady. Not the day before the damn event proper."

Hannah shook her head. As far as she was concerned, her aunt was worrying over nothing.

"In fact…" Dorothy threw her hands in the air. "You may as well give up now. Honestly, you're not going to finish."

"Of course I'm going to finish."

"I don't think you will," Mel said.

"As much as it pains me to say it, I don't think you will either," Liv said. "Not the way you're going."

Hannah couldn't believe what she was hearing. After all the work she'd put in, no way was she pulling out without trying. Insulted by the mere suggestion, they might not have much faith in her, but that didn't stop Hannah having faith in herself. "I'll bet you anything I cross that finishing line before either of you two." She turned to Dorothy. "Take note, Team Leader. *Anything.*"

Dorothy sighed. "See what I mean. There's no talking to her."

"I don't mind a bit of fighting talk," Mel said, her competitive streak coming to the fore. "But when you say 'anything', I hope you're a woman of your word."

"Of course I am." Hannah felt affronted *anyone* would think otherwise, let alone one of her best friends.

Dorothy, Mel and Liv shared a look, as if they were suddenly all thinking the same thing. They turned to Hannah, each of them wearing a mischievous smile.

"You're on," Dorothy said.

"If you don't finish this race before me and Liv," Mel said. "You're to speak to Gabe and find out what the real story is behind this wife business."

He was the last person Hannah wanted to converse with. She opened her mouth to protest, but Liv stopped her.

"And if things aren't what they seem, you're to go on a date with him."

Realising she'd been set up, Hannah had to remind herself that a bet was a bet. She narrowed her eyes, and her gaze went from one woman to the next and to the next.

"A proper date," all three of them said.

CHAPTER 44

RACE DAY

*H*aving woken early, Hannah had lain in the quiet for what felt like forever. She'd tried getting back to sleep, but her nerves over the day ahead wouldn't let her. She grabbed her pillow, gave it a good plump, and threw her head back down for the millionth time. After a while, Hannah groaned, and whipping her duvet back, decided she may as well get up.

Grabbing her dressing gown, she retrieved her phone from the bedside cabinet, stuffing it into her pocket as she made her way downstairs. Tiptoeing as she went so as not to wake Dorothy, as Hannah entered the kitchen, she was surprised to find her aunt already sat there.

Hands wrapped around a mug, Dorothy looked up. "You couldn't sleep either?"

Hannah headed for the kettle. "Fresh cup of tea?"

"Ooh, yes please. This one's cold."

"Can you believe it's race day already?" Hannah waited for an answer and when one didn't come she paused in her actions. She turned to her aunt, concerned. "Is everything all right?"

"I'm just thinking." Dorothy sighed. "About how after today, it'll be time for me to go back to Norfolk."

Having not previously joined the dots, Hannah supposed that made sense. Dorothy's stay had sort of come to a natural end. However, suddenly feeling as miserable as Dorothy looked, Hannah wished it hadn't. In those last few weeks, Hannah had enjoyed Dorothy's company more than she could have anticipated. Her aunt might not have been a guest for long in the bigger scheme of things, but Hannah knew not having her around would take some getting used to. "You don't have to go just yet, do you?"

"I'll have to at some point."

"Not necessarily," Hannah replied.

Hannah might not have wanted to think about Gabe, but she couldn't help but consider his living arrangements. Gabe and Roger, just like Hannah and Dorothy, were two different generations and they seemed to make things work. It wasn't as if Hannah didn't have the room for Dorothy to stay for as long as she liked. Of course there was Beth and Archie to consider, but Hannah was sure they'd love Dorothy as much as she did.

"What do you mean?"

"I mean you're welcome to stay longer. Who knows, you might decide not to go back to Norfolk at all."

For the first time since landing, Dorothy appeared lost for words.

"Don't make any decisions now," Hannah said. "Take your time. Think about what you want."

Hannah's mobile rang. Pulling it from her dressing gown pocket her eyes widened in surprise. "It's Beth and Archie." France might be an hour ahead, but it was early on the other side of the channel too. "Seems like we're not the only ones who couldn't sleep."

"You take the call, I'll make the tea," Dorothy said.

As Hannah moved to leave the room, she felt her aunt take hold of her arm.

"And thank you," Dorothy said. "That was very kind what you said just then."

Despite appreciating the sentiment, Hannah saw no need for gratitude. "I'm only saying it like it is."

Leaving her aunt on kettle duty, Hannah made her way into the lounge. Propping up her phone, she clicked to answer. As Beth and Archie appeared on the screen, Hannah settled down ready to chat.

"Hi, Mum," Beth and Archie said.

Hannah frowned. "Where are you?" Clearly not at the villa they'd rented, she took in their surroundings. With lots of French chatter taking place, people passed by with cups of coffee, glasses of juice, muffins and pain au chocolat.

"On our way to Paris," Beth said, excited.

Hannah swooned in envy. She readily envisaged the early-morning swirling mists of the River Seine and could see herself strolling along Paris's wide tree-lined avenues, admiring lavish formal gardens. In her imagination she sat under sparkling sunshine on the café terraces of Boulevard Saint-Germain. Hannah would have given anything to ride the lift to the top of the Eiffel Tower where she could soak up the breathtaking Parisian cityscape with its criss-crossing boulevards and historic monuments, cathedral, and basilicas. "I'm so jealous of you right now, you wouldn't believe."

Archie laughed. "Dad said it would be a waste if we didn't go. Seeing as we're in France anyway."

Hannah didn't often agree with Carl but on that occasion, she most definitely did.

"We were actually ringing to wish you good luck," Beth said. "For the race."

"Aw, you remembered."

211

"According to Dad, we're going to be on the road for a while, so we might not get the chance later."

"France *is* a big country," Hannah said.

"And of course, once we get to Paris we'll be too busy," Beth said. "I mean there's the Musée du Louvre, the Champs-Élysées, the Arc de Triomphe…" She sighed. "We've got so much to see."

"As long as we don't have to go on a Seine river cruise." Archie grimaced. "After being on that catamaran, I'm done with boats."

Hannah tried and failed to keep a straight face. She still hadn't got over them being seasick on calm waters. "Make sure you think of me, struggling to run and breathe at the same time, while you're both admiring the Mona Lisa or wandering around the Notre Dame."

"We will," Beth said.

"I wish we could be there," Archie said. "I don't think I've ever seen you run."

Knowing he was being cheeky, Hannah laughed. "Believe me, you'd remember if you had."

Beth glanced over at something off screen. She nodded. "Sorry, Mum, but we've got to go. Dad's just told us to hurry up."

"Well thank you for ringing."

"You do know we're proud of you for doing this, Mum, don't you?" Archie said.

"Because you should," Beth added.

"I do." If she was honest, she was proud of herself.

Taking in her children's sincerity, Hannah didn't know if it was that, the race, the upset she'd experienced of late, or a mix of all three, but she suddenly felt overwhelmed and tears threatened her eyes.

Hannah made sure to smile, doing her best not to let Beth and Archie see her distress. "Now go on," she said to them. "Enjoy Paris."

CHAPTER 45

"*Just send the letter through and we'll deal with its contents.*"

Pacing up and down in the back garden, in the space of one phone call, Gabe felt the weight he'd been carrying around lift.

"*We'll talk more once I've established what we're dealing with.*"

"Brilliant," Gabe said. "And thanks for speaking to me on a Saturday. It's much appreciated."

"*No problem. I was working anyway. Besides, any friend of Quentin's is a friend of mine. I'll be in touch, yeah?*"

"Look forward to it." Ending the call, Gabe took a deep breath and exhaled. A part of him wanted to mark the occasion. It was, after all, the end of a sorry era. But how could he do something positive when underneath it all he felt anything but. The only person he'd want to celebrate with regardless was Hannah.

Heading back inside, he glanced over at the kitchen counter where Kate's letter continued to lay unopened. Thanks to Quentin's contact, whatever was in it was now in the hands of Washington, Greenway, and Forbes. From that moment on, he had no reason to see Kate ever again. Anything she had to say, she could say via the solicitor he'd just instructed. Grateful to his mate for recommending him, Gabe made a mental note to buy Quentin a pint the next time he saw him.

Putting his phone in his shirt pocket, Gabe knew as far as Hannah was concerned it was too little, too late. Of course, Hannah had every right to view him as the lowest of the low, but the last thing Gabe had wanted to do was hurt her. Moreover, as much as he wanted to put all the blame for Hannah's upset on Kate, he knew he couldn't. Rather, he should have been honest about his situation from the start.

Gabe frowned, wondering why he'd acted like such an ostrich and buried his head in the sand. When it came to his and Kate's relationship, he shouldn't have left it up to Kate to decide when they got divorced, he should have taken control. He should have filed for it, and a long time ago.

"Sorted?" Roger asked, as he entered the room.

"Finally," Gabe replied.

"Good lad." Roger checked his watch. "Does this mean we can leave now? Hannah's race'll be getting underway soon."

"You head off," Gabe replied. "I'm not going. She won't want me there."

Roger frowned. "You don't know that."

Gabe scoffed. "You didn't see her face when Kate turned up."

"I'll never understand what you saw in that woman."

As Roger shook his head in disdain, the last thing Gabe needed was an *I told you so.* "Not helpful, Dad."

"So, that's it, is it? You're just giving up on Hannah?" Roger asked. "She doesn't get an apology, an explanation, the chance to slap you in the face for being so stupid?"

Knowing he more than deserved a slap, Gabe recalled the ignored phone calls he'd made and the unanswered messages he'd sent. There were so many, he was on the verge of looking like a stalker. "She doesn't want to speak to me."

"What do you expect?" Roger stared at Gabe like he was an

idiot. "The girl's had a shock. She's upset. But that doesn't mean you don't try. And before you say anything, phone calls and texts don't cut it. If you truly are sorry, son, you'll look her in the eye and say it."

As hard as it was to hear, Gabe knew his dad was right. "Okay, you win."

Roger smiled. "Does that mean…?"

Having supported Hannah through her running journey thus far, Gabe wanted nothing more than to be there when she crossed the finish line. Even if he ended up doing it from afar on account of her telling him where to go. Already short for time, he grabbed his car keys off the side. "It does."

As he headed for the door, he paused and turned to Roger, who he suddenly saw as dawdling. "Are you coming, or what?"

CHAPTER 46

"Look at all these people," Hannah said to her aunt and Mel.

"Isn't it wonderful?" Aunt Dorothy said.

"I can't wait to get going," Mel said.

Carrying a deckchair for Dorothy to sit on once the race got underway, Hannah proudly sported her numbered bib as she soaked up the atmosphere and took in her fellow competitors. As everyone around them chatted, the air buzzed with excitement.

The more serious of those taking part were already stretching and limbering up ready to beat their personal bests, while others took a more relaxed approach having brought their dogs along as running companions. Glancing around, Hannah thanked goodness she'd upped her fitness level. Even the pensioners amongst them appeared to be in good athletic shape. "I hope Liv can find us in the middle of this lot."

"She can't miss us wearing these," Mel said. Thanks to their bright pink T-shirts, there was no denying the three of them stood out.

Wethersham Hall's estate was vast and after checking in, like everyone else it seemed, Hannah's group had decided to meet at the Rotunda café, which wasn't far from the race's start line. A circular stone building, it had a wide shuttered window that operated as a serving hatch and white bistro sets were dotted around its exterior providing seating for its customers. With the race due to start and her nerves coming to the fore, were it not for their team bet, Hannah would have been tempted to grab a coffee and watch events instead of seeing the race through.

"If you want to back out, now's the time to do it," Mel said, clearly exploiting Hannah's trepidation. Reaching into her pocket, Mel pulled out her Saint Hilda's long-distance running medal and dangled it in front of Hannah. "Bearing in mind you're up against some stiff competition."

"Exactly," Dorothy said. "Why not admit defeat and save yourself the pain."

"And embarrassment," Mel said, tucking her medal away again.

Hannah shook her head. "It's going to be like that, is it?" Unable to help but smile, she couldn't believe they were resorting to mind games.

Dorothy sniggered.

"Let's see who's laughing come the finishing line, shall we?" Hannah said, more than up for the challenge.

"There you all are!"

Hannah spun round to see Liv, with Quentin in tow, fast approaching. Unlike Hannah, who wore her trusty leggings and team T-shirt, Liv looked the real deal in her blue running shorts and light-grey singlet tank top. Her hair was tied into a neat bun at the back of her head, and she had a sweatband on one wrist and stats monitor on the other.

Hannah indicated Liv's ensemble. "I see you mean business too." Hannah's gaze flitted between her and Mel. "Let's hope you're both better at running than you are at psychology warfare. Although I have to say, Liv, I'm a bit disappointed you're not wearing pink."

Liv nodded to Quentin, who reached into the rucksack he carried. Producing not one, but two team T-shirts, he and Liv proceeded to put them on.

Mel suddenly froze, her expression serious.

"What is it?" Hannah stiffened in response to Mel. She wore the same expression that Gabe had worn when Kate made her surprise appearance.

"Russel?" Mel said, unsure.

Hannah turned. Taking in the red hair and black-framed glasses, she'd have recognised Russel's steely stare anywhere. As her eyes went from him to Mel and back again, her heart did a little dance on her friend's behalf.

Russel's sudden arrival seemed to impact everyone. Dorothy oohed and Liv aahed, and even Quentin appeared to swoon. He wrapped an arm around Liv's shoulder and pulled her close. Hannah couldn't help but feel a bit envious.

Seeing Mel and Russel look as unsure as each other, Hannah sighed, wistful. It seemed her friend had been right to previously say things weren't always as they seem. With Mel stood as if unable to move Hannah nudged her forward.

Mel continued to appear hesitant, but thanks to everyone's encouraging nods she finally stepped forward. Hannah and the others took a couple of paces back, at the same time turning away to give Mel and Russel some privacy.

Despite being pleased for her friends, Hannah felt sad for herself. She had Dorothy for support, of course, but it would have been nice to have Beth and Archie there too. Consoling herself with the fact that they'd made a point of calling to wish her luck, Hannah just hoped they'd be as proud of her come the end of the race as they'd been at the beginning.

A picture of Gabe popped into her head and as angry as she was with the man, Hannah couldn't one hundred per cent deny that his presence was also missed. She glanced around, secretly hoping she might experience her own romantic gesture.

Deflated, Gabe was nowhere in sight. Hannah felt Dorothy's, Liv's and Quentin's eyes on her. "What?" she asked, returning their stares.

"Makes you think, doesn't it?" Dorothy said. "Seeing those two."

Hannah snuck a peek at Mel and Russel. Talking over each other, they both seemed to be apologising for their part in the misunderstanding. Hannah's situation with Gabe, however, was different. There was no misunderstanding. Not only was Gabe married, he hadn't bothered to inform her of the fact. "Not really, no," Hannah flatly replied.

"Who's the red-haired geek?" Francesca asked. Appearing as if from nowhere, like Liv, she was dressed to win.

"If you're talking about Russel," Hannah replied. "That's Mel's boyfriend."

"Mel has a boyfriend? Since when?" Shaking herself out of her confusion, Francesca spotted Quentin and came over all coy. "And who is this lovely gentleman?"

Recalling how Francesca had fluttered her lashes at Gabe, Hannah wondered if the woman had any shame.

Quentin stepped forward to shake Francesca's hand. "Quentin."

Francesca's eyes lit up at his touch. "Pleased to meet you, I'm sure."

Quentin let go and immediately put his arm around Liv's shoulders. "*Liv's* boyfriend."

The more Hannah saw of Quentin, the more she liked him.

"Really?" Francesca let out a laugh as she looked straight at Liv. "How did you manage to pull *him*?"

Liv opened her mouth to speak but was saved from herself when a voice spoke over a tannoy.

"Could all competitors please make your way to the starting line."

Francesca flicked her ponytail. "Sounds like that's our cue."

Mel hastened over. "Aunt Dorothy, is it all right if Russel stays with you? It's his first visit here and he doesn't know anyone. This time he might really get lost."

Hannah didn't think she'd ever seen Mel's smile so bright.

"Of course, it is," Dorothy replied. "Once you're off and running, we'll head for the finishing line and wait for you there." She turned to Russel. "Won't we?"

Russel's eyes widened as he looked around in awe. "I feel like an extra in *Chariots of Fire*."

"Oh, I love that film," Dorothy said.

Mel gave Dorothy the biggest of hugs. "Thank you."

"You're coming too, aren't you, Quentin?" Dorothy asked.

Quentin was too busy kissing Liv good luck to answer.

"Guys," Hannah said. "Time to let go."

Hannah handed Quentin her aunt's deckchair. Leaving him, her aunt and Russel to head off, she felt nervous as she, Mel and Liv followed the crowd. Despite her prior confidence, Hannah hoped she'd done enough training to finish the race, let alone beat Mel and Liv.

At last coming to a standstill, it was clear the serious athletes had been given pole position at the front, something Hannah was glad about. The circuit was primarily through woodland and worried she'd stray off into the middle of nowhere, having someone to follow gave her a better chance of staying on track. Hannah took a deep breath and checking her watch, saw it was race time. "Good luck, ladies," she said.

"You too," Mel and Liv chorused.

"Luck has nothing to do with it," Francesca said.

CHAPTER 47

$\mathcal{A}$s she waited for the race to start, Hannah warmed up with her usual tricep stretches and side lunges. She jumped up and down and jiggled her body to loosen herself up. Anxious to start with, Hannah stopped still and her nerves increased when the organiser's voice suddenly sounded on the tannoy. Hannah took a deep breath before giving her team mates a quick thumbs up.

"On your marks," he said.

Hannah quickly positioned herself accordingly.

"Get set."

She dug her leading foot into the ground in readiness.

The starting pistol fired.

Hannah propelled herself forward and with Wethersham Hall behind her, set off on a jog down its tree-lined avenue. She didn't care that Mel, Liv, and Francesca were racing ahead. Preferring a steadier start, Hannah had a plan. In her mind, if she conserved enough energy, she'd not only finish the race, but would overtake her team members one by one when she completed the last leg with a sprint.

As Hannah settled into her own pace, she couldn't believe

how quickly race day had come around. It didn't seem two minutes since Beth and Archie had left for France, and Liv was suggesting she, Hannah and Mel sign up. Hannah had hoped Carl would arrange an earlier ferry home, so Beth and Archie could be there to cheer her on in person. However, Hannah pushed her disappointment aside, and keeping her head up and chest out, told herself it was only right they got to enjoy the last couple of days of their holiday.

Hannah followed the runners ahead when they took a right and after a short distance picked up a path that hugged a huge expanse of playing fields. Hannah had done all her training on either concrete or the treadmill and running on grass was a different experience. The shock that usually ran through her feet and up to her knees was less impacting thanks to the softer surface and while running had consistently given Hannah the headspace to think, without traffic and meandering pedestrians to consider, she was pleased to find her mind felt even freer.

A fellow competitor overtook Hannah.

"Good luck," the woman shouted as she passed by.

Hannah called after her. "You too!"

Other than beating Mel and Liv, Hannah didn't care where she placed. The fact that she was taking part in the race at all was something to be proud of. In the space of a few weeks, it was as if she'd become a different person. She'd got fitter; she'd mooted a new direction workwise; acknowledged it was time to give Beth and Archie more responsibility; and for a short while, had even considered opening herself up romantically. Hannah frowned. Until Gabe had reminded her that matters of the heart brought nothing but misery.

Hannah glanced over her shoulder, pleased to see she'd got round three sides of the parkland. But her positivity was interrupted when she began to feel the burn in her legs. Her muscles had clearly worked harder than usual due to the undulating fields.

She reached a bridge and leaving the grass behind, ran onto a trail that cut through woodland. Aware that this was the longest stretch of the run, the light dappled around her, and the terrain grew even more uneven, which wasn't just tiring, it put pressure on Hannah's weak ankle. Forced to constantly negotiate the rocks and logs that lay in her path, while avoiding overgrown nettles and scrub, Hannah had to concentrate on her environment as much as she did her breathing. It would have been easy to compensate by slowing down, but Hannah knew she couldn't afford to. If she didn't keep up her pace, she'd never overtake Liv and Mel. No way was she losing their bet.

Hannah's foot caught in a pothole, and she yelped as she tumbled forward. She put her arms out to break her fall, wincing as her palms slapped the ground. A searing pain shot through her ankle.

"Jesus! Are you okay?" another runner said, stopping to help.

Hannah hauled herself up into a seated position, and pushing her fringe away from her face, gave the good Samaritan a fake smile. "I'm fine, thank you. I just tripped. Don't let me stop you. You go, finish the race."

The good Samaritan didn't appear convinced.

"Honestly, I'll be all right when I get my breath back."

"Are you sure?"

Thankfully Hannah was at last taken at her word and the good Samaritan headed off.

Left to her own devices, Hannah cautiously wiggled her foot. Her ankle hurt, but the fact that it moved without making her scream told Hannah it wasn't broken. Looking around at the leafy wilderness, she wanted to cry. She pulled her phone from her pocket ready to ring for help, before staring at the shattered screen. Tapping it regardless, she tried to get into her contact list, but to no avail. Hannah's shoulders slumped. Wanting to cry even more, it seemed she was on her own.

Hannah knew she couldn't sit there all day, and careful not to further injure herself, she managed to haul herself back onto her feet. She took a step forward, but flinching, quickly realised she wasn't going to get very far unaided.

She glanced around the woodland floor until her eyes settled on a broken branch. Hopping over, Hannah balanced herself as best she could as she picked it up and tore off its excess twigs. Testing the branch out for size, she insisted it would make the perfect crutch. Tears finally sprung in her eyes as her predicament set in.

Hannah had been looking forward to showing Beth and Archie her medal when they got home from France, but after falling there was no way she could finish the race in the allotted time to get one. Hannah whimpered. No way could she win her bet.

She took a deep breath and despite everything, a determination suddenly swept over her. "One thing you can do." Hannah mustered every ounce of willpower she had. "Is finish this damn race."

CHAPTER 48

"Come on, Dad. We're gonna miss all the action."

As they made their way through groups of spectators, Gabe hurried Roger along. Getting to the other side of town on a Saturday lunchtime had been difficult enough, but Gabe hadn't anticipated the added trouble it took finding a parking space once they'd arrived at Wethersham Hall. The hour-long race was well underway and, no doubt, runners were already crossing the finishing line. Gabe wouldn't have been surprised if Hannah was one of them. He knew she'd trained hard and was more than capable of smashing it.

"There they are," Roger said. His face lit up as he spotted a grouping of pink T-shirts.

Following his dad's gaze, Gabe clocked Dorothy sat in a deckchair with her knitting resting on her lap. Quentin was with her, and forced to squint, Gabe felt sure he recognised the third person in the group. "Of course. Mel's photo," he said, pleasantly surprised.

With no sign of Hannah, Mel or Liv, Gabe took a deep breath to compose himself. He felt a mix of nervousness and hope. Nerves because there was a good chance Hannah would soon tell him to go away and never come back. Hope because Russel had clearly turned out to be a good guy and not a baddie. If that didn't tell Hannah things weren't always what they seemed, then nothing would.

"Gabe!" Dorothy called out. Dropping her knitting into her bag, she rose to her feet and stepped forward to hug him. "I'm so glad you came."

"Me too, mate. Liv would've been fuming if you hadn't." Quentin laughed as he hugged Gabe. "I'd have never heard the end of it."

Dorothy encouraged Russel forward. "Gabe, this is Russel. Russel, Gabe."

Gabe shook Russel's hand. "Good to meet you, at last."

"Likewise."

"And this is Roger," Dorothy said. "Who makes the best risotto on the planet."

Gabe checked his watch. With not much race time left, he addressed the others. "They should be coming into view soon."

Quentin grew excited. "I think Liv and Mel are heading this way now." He nodded toward the woodland's edge, where two bright pink T-shirts could be seen in the distance. He put his hands either side of his mouth. "Come on, Liv!" Quentin shouted.

Russel joined in. "Almost there, Mel."

Gabe put his fingers to his lips and whistled, and along with the rest of the group, raucously cheered them towards the finishing line.

Mel and Liv looked elated yet shattered as they made their way along the final stretch. Crossing the line, they hugged each other and when one of the race organisers stepped forward to put their medals around their necks, Mel and Liv jumped up and down to celebrate their win.

"Well done, babe," Quentin said.

As Mel and Liv approached, Liv broke into a run and jumping

into Quentin's arms, she wrapped her legs around him. The two of them kissed long and hard.

Gabe watched Quentin spin Liv around, while Russel took Mel's hand and gave her a quick kiss on the cheek. Gabe felt a pang of jealousy, knowing the way things were between him and Hannah, she wouldn't appreciate either gesture from him.

"Am I glad that's over with," Liv said, her feet back on terra firma. "Please tell me we've beaten Francesca." Her eyes widened in anticipation.

Aunt Dorothy shook her head. "Afraid not. She came through about ten minutes ago."

"You mean she took her medal and left? She didn't stay to cheer the rest of us in?" Liv scoffed. "How's that for team work?"

Mel glanced around the group. "No Hannah yet?" Realising they'd won the bet, she looked from Liv to Dorothy. "You know what this means, don't you."

Gabe frowned, wondering where Hannah could be. He put a hand up to protect his eyes from the sun as he focused on the racetrack, but she was nowhere in sight. "I hope she's okay."

"She'll be fine," Roger said, not looking quite as convinced as he sounded.

"I hope she hasn't got lost," Mel said.

"I must admit, I'm surprised she's not here yet," Dorothy said. "I know from her training sessions she can run faster than this."

Gabe continued to stare into the distance. "Do you think we should phone her?" Without waiting for an answer, he pulled out his mobile and clicked to call. "That's strange," he said, as the ringtone continued. "She's not answering."

"Maybe she doesn't have signal," Mel said, hopeful.

"Maybe." Gabe finally let his hand drop and he turned to the others. "I think I'll have a wander. Just to put my mind at ease."

CHAPTER 49

$\mathcal{H}$annah tried to remain dignified as she hobbled along. The number of runners passing by might have dwindled to dribs and drabs, but they continued to overtake. Hannah forced herself to look cheerful with every enquiry into her welfare, encouraging each good Samaritan to carry on without *her* or worry. However, trekking along the woodland trail with an injured ankle and a makeshift crutch was both embarrassing and painful.

Hannah knew it would be easy to drop to the ground and break down in tears. "You've got this," she insisted, over and over. Despite her slow progress, she refused to give in.

After a time, Hannah's competitors stopped appearing and it became clear she would, without doubt, place last. That was if the organisers weren't already packing up ready to go home along with everyone else. Then she wouldn't place at all.

Spotting a fallen tree, Hannah decided to rest her ankle for a moment, and limping over, she perched on its thick gnarled trunk. She considered the ride she'd been on those last weeks. Looking down at her injured ankle, Hannah knew that learning to run and breathe at the same time was the least of the lessons she'd learned.

She smiled. Some of the past month had been good, like getting to know Aunt Dorothy again.

Her smiled drooped. Some of it uncomfortable, like having to recognise it was time to broaden her horizons and set herself a new challenge. For her own sake as much as Beth and Archie's. Hannah knew she'd micro-managed every aspect of their lives for far too long. She had to start delegating.

Hannah's smile disappeared completely. Then there was the downright bad. Hannah appreciated Dorothy's pep talk about forcing herself into difficult situations but when Carl had ended their marriage, Hannah had vowed never to let anyone hurt her again. If that meant closing herself off from matters of the heart, then that was what she had to do.

She pictured Beth and Archie as young children. Back then keeping her pledge had been simple. Her children's needs came above all else and Hannah had had neither the time nor inclination to think about her own; a situation that she happily let continue. Then along came their trip to France, turning Hannah's well-oiled routine and single status mindset into disarray.

"Hannah!"

She looked up to see Gabe, like a knight in shining armour, racing towards her. Her heart leapt but bringing it back to reality with a bump, her head told it to get a grip. That man had caused her the biggest turmoil of all.

"What happened?" Gabe asked.

As if her outstretched leg and makeshift crutch weren't enough of a clue, Hannah frowned. "What do you think happened?" Convinced Gabe wore a hint of amusement as he plonked himself down next to her on the tree trunk, Hannah wondered what was so funny.

He indicated her foot. "Does it hurt?"

Another ridiculous question, Hannah considered. "Again, what do you think?"

A part of her felt bad for snapping at Gabe, but Hannah couldn't seem to help herself. The last thing she wanted to do was join in with his idle chit-chat. In fact, as they both fell into silence, she didn't want to talk to him at all.

"It's not what you're imagining," Gabe said, at last breaking the quiet.

Knowing he was referring to his relationship with Kate, Hannah recalled the conditions of her bet with Dorothy, Mel, and Liv. She sighed. As a woman of her word, Hannah knew she'd have to listen to what Gabe had to say at some point, so she decided to get it out of the way.

"I don't need to use my imagination, Gabe. Kate was very clear about who she is."

"But that's what I'm saying, Hannah. It's not what you think."

With the man talking in riddles, Hannah's frustration grew. "So the two of you aren't married?"

"No." Gabe paused. "Well, technically, yes."

Hannah wished he'd make his mind up. "It's not a trick question. You either are or you aren't."

"Put it this way, we're not divorced."

Staring down at his hands, Gabe appeared as uncomfortable as Hannah felt. "You really aren't making much sense."

"I suppose what I'm trying to say is, Kate and I might still be married on paper, but that's it. We split up a couple of years ago. Until she turned up the other night, I hadn't seen her since. She moved away and after a while, I moved on. I had no idea she was even in town."

Hannah scoffed. Having seen Kate's name pop up on his phone, Hannah wasn't about to accept that so readily. "And the calls?"

Finally, Gabe looked at Hannah. "What calls?"

Hannah raised her eyebrows. "The demanding client who happens to have the same name as your ex?"

"Oh." Gabe sighed. "Those calls." He twisted round on the trunk, angling himself towards Hannah. "You have to understand, for me, Kate's decision to leave came from nowhere. At the time, I was devastated. I didn't think I'd ever get over her."

Thanks to Carl, Hannah understood that feeling all too well.

"Although now I can see she did me a favour, back then I was gutted. I suppose I didn't want old wounds being ripped open again, if that makes sense?" He sounded desperate for Hannah to believe him. "It seemed easier to ignore her and hope she'd stop calling. That she'd just go away." Gabe sighed. "I got that wrong, didn't I?"

"Does that mean you still have feelings for her?"

Gabe let out a laugh. "Absolutely not."

"Does she still have feelings for you?" After all, Hannah considered, Kate had reappeared in his life for a reason.

Gabe shook his head. "The only person Kate's ever cared about is Kate."

"So why is she here?" Kate's presence continued to make no sense. "Why come back now?"

Gabe scoffed. "She wants a divorce." Suddenly serious again, he stared at Hannah. "Remember when Aunt Dorothy asked me if there was a Mrs Gabe and I said no."

How could Hannah forget? It was that that had made Kate's appearance such a shock.

"It wasn't a lie, not really. My marriage to Kate ended a long time ago. A piece of paper means nothing." He paused for a moment. "I'm sorry I wasn't upfront about everything. You shouldn't have had to find out about Kate the way you did."

Appreciating the apology, Hannah felt herself soften towards Gabe. "You could have told me, you know. After what I went through with Carl, I'd have understood. Maybe not the fact that neither of you had bothered to properly finalise things. But as for the rest of it."

Gabe straightened himself up. "At least now you know all there is to know."

Hannah took a deep breath and exhaled.

Gabe looked at Hannah, hopeful. "So where does that leave us?"

It was Hannah's turn to laugh. "Us? You're being a bit presumptuous, aren't you?"

Gabe scoffed. "And you're doing what you once accused me of."

Hannah didn't follow.

"Deflecting," Gabe said. "Answering my question with a question." He rose to his feet. "We should go. Everyone will be worried."

Seeing him hold out his hands to help pull her up, Hannah couldn't help but see his gesture as a kind of déjà vu. It was as if they'd come full circle and were back to when they'd first properly met. Happy to accept his help, she wondered if they really could start again. Was life truly that simple? Once on her feet, she reached for her makeshift crutch.

Gabe took it from her. "You don't need that."

Hannah looked at him confused, wondering how she was supposed to walk without it. "But…"

Before she could finish her sentence, Gabe had reached down and wrapped his arms around her thighs. She screamed as he hoisted her up. "What are you doing?" Before Hannah knew it, he'd swung her over his shoulder into a fireman's lift.

"What does it look like?" Gabe replied, laughing. "I'm helping you finish the race."

CHAPTER 50

"*A*re you okay up there?" Gabe asked.

Hannah howled with laughter. Despite the feel of Gabe's firm arms gripping her thighs, she bounded about as they went. Gabe might have been a fitness freak, but she wasn't the slimmest of women. She didn't know how he managed to keep her on his shoulders. "More importantly, are you?"

The dirt track turned grassy indicating they'd, at last, cleared the woodland. As well as seeing the ground beneath his feet, Hannah had the perfect view of what she considered Gabe's rather nice backside, but not much else. She cocked her head at the faint sound of shouting and whistling. "I take it that means we're almost there?"

"We certainly are. Thank goodness."

Feeling sorry for the man, Hannah wasn't surprised to hear his voice starting to strain.

As the commotion got louder, Hannah had a good idea who was responsible, and she easily pictured Aunt Dorothy, Mel and Liv jumping up and down, all the while willing Gabe towards them.

It wasn't long before the cheering intensified, and Hannah

and Gabe found themselves surrounded by pink T-shirts. The excitement was deafening and, despite being crushed in the melee, Gabe eased Hannah off his shoulders. He puffed and panted while Hannah struggled to keep her balance thanks to her injured foot. She couldn't help but wince at the pain.

"Oh my word," Dorothy said. Seeing Hannah's plight, she grabbed her deckchair. "Here, sit down."

Doing as she was told, Hannah took in her enthusiastic welcome party. While not surprised that everyone had waited for her, she wouldn't have blamed them if they'd gone home. Her eyes widened and her heart screamed. "Beth! Archie!" Taking in her children, her eyes filled with tears.

"Hello, Mum," they said. Grinning, they threw themselves at Hannah and wrapping their arms around her, squeezed her tight.

Hannah pulled back to get a good look at them. With their sun-kissed locks and gorgeous tans, they appeared older. Hannah was convinced they'd grown. "But how? This morning you were in France."

"We were at Calais, waiting to get on the ferry," Beth said.

"You didn't really think we'd miss your race, did you?" Archie asked.

"But what about Paris?"

Beth wrinkled her nose. "We made it up."

"We wanted to surprise you," Archie said. "Dad's gonna ring you later. He and Monica headed home after dropping us off."

Hannah pulled her children close. Hugging them tight for a second time, she didn't want to let them go. "Thank you. You don't know how much this means."

"Mum, we can't breathe," they said, making everyone else laugh.

Releasing them, Hannah looked from her children to the rest of the group.

"We're so proud of you," Liv said, standing there with Quentin's arm around the back of her shoulders.

Mel held Russel's hand. "I second that."

Dorothy put a hand on her chest and Hannah was convinced she was about to cry. "And I third it."

Hannah chuckled as she turned her attention back to Beth and Archie, still unable to believe they were right there in front of her.

Finally, Hannah looked at Gabe, who gave her a wink. Her tummy tingled and for the first time since meeting Gabe, she embraced the sensation.

"Time to get that ankle seen to," he said.

Hannah squealed and the rest of the group cheered when in one swift movement Gabe reached down, picked Hannah up and again threw her over his shoulder.

"Three cheers for Hannah!" Liv shouted, as Gabe carried her off.

"Hip, hip, hooray," her friends and family chorused, as everyone headed towards the car park.

CHAPTER 51

*H*aving never known her children be so quiet, Hannah wondered what they were up to. Not sure what to expect, she took in the sight before her as she entered the living room.

Aunt Dorothy sat in the middle of the sofa, with Beth on one side of her and Archie on the other. It seemed Dorothy was teaching them both to knit, and concentrating like never before, Beth and Archie methodically wound lengths of wool around their needles.

Hannah took a moment to watch them, glad that Dorothy had decided not to rush back to Norfolk. No long-term plans had been made, but she was happy for now. Pleased Beth and Archie were home where they belonged, Hannah had been right to think they'd love her aunt as much she did.

Hannah coughed and thinking it a shame to interrupt them, they all glanced up. "So, will I do?"

Dorothy's face broke into a grin. "Gorgeous. As always."

Beth shook her head. "I can't believe how different you look."

"That's exercise for you," Archie said. "And a bit of make-up. Oh, and some new clothes."

Hannah laughed. "Cheeky!"

Holding wisps of hair to stop them dangling in front of her eyes, Hannah glanced down at her red maxi wrap dress and white trainers. "You can see why I feel both over and underdressed at the same time."

"Well, you will injure your ankle," Dorothy said.

"I wouldn't worry, it's fashionable, Mum," Beth said.

Hannah was impressed. Fashionable wasn't a word Beth usually ascribed to her.

A car horn beeped, and Hannah's gaze flew to the window. She hesitated. She hadn't been on a date since being with Carl, and having kept a lid on her anxiety all day, it suddenly came to the fore.

"A bet's a bet," Dorothy said, reminding Hannah that she didn't have a choice.

"I'm not backing out," Hannah said. "I'm just nervous."

Beth laughed. "It's not like you've got anything to worry about. It's obvious Gabe's mad about you."

"He'd have to be to carry you on his shoulder all that way," Archie said. "I wouldn't have done it."

"That's because you're not strong enough," Beth said.

Shaking her head and chuckling, Hannah grabbed her handbag. "Behave for Aunt Dorothy," she said, as she headed for the front door. "And I won't be late," she called out, shutting it behind her.

Making her way down the garden path, Hannah took in Gabe's smile as she approached. She blushed as his eyes widened in appreciation. He stood, casually leaning against the passenger side of his car looking every inch the Greek god she'd come to expect. Hannah couldn't fail to notice he also smelt divine as he leaned in and kissed her cheek.

"Your carriage awaits," he said. Opening the door so she could climb in, Gabe let Hannah get settled before closing it and heading round to the driver's side. "Good to see you made an effort for me," he said, putting his keys in the ignition.

Again feeling her cheeks redden, Hannah playfully tapped his arm. "I'm not dressed like this for you." She made a show of sticking her nose in the air. "It's for me."

"Why do I believe you?" Gabe said, his grin continuing long after he'd started up the engine and pulled away.

"I still don't see why you can't tell me where we're going," Hannah said, eager to find out. "It's only fair I know what I'm letting myself in for."

"If I did, it wouldn't be a surprise."

"What if I don't like surprises?"

"Trust me, you'll like this one."

With no other choice, Hannah stared out of the window, looking for clues that might reveal where they were headed. Unfortunately for her, none seemed to be forthcoming. "Come on, Gabe. Tell me." She fluttered her eyelashes. "Please."

The man remained silent.

Finally, he pulled off the main road and Hannah figured it out. Hannah straightened up in her seat. Having taken that very turn many times herself over the years, she, Beth and Archie had enjoyed many a lakeside picnic. "What're we doing here?"

Driving down towards the water, Hannah wondered if Gabe had thought on similar lines and arranged an evening of al fresco dining. Unable to imagine anything more romantic, she craned her neck to look through the windscreen hoping to spot a blanket, with food and glasses of wine ready and waiting. As Gabe brought the car to a standstill and turned off the engine, Hannah felt bewildered.

There was nothing. All she could see was grass and water.

"Come on," Gabe said, seeming excited to get going.

With her curiosity growing, Hannah climbed out too. She watched Gabe head to the rear of the vehicle and opening the boot, pull out a picnic basket and blanket. Hannah smiled, glad to see she was right.

Leaving the basket and blanket by the car, Gabe took Hannah's hand and led her to the water's edge. "Ta Da!" he said. Throwing his arms out wide, he waited for her reaction.

Confused, Hannah wondered what she was supposed to be looking at. All she could see was a rowing boat.

Hannah's eyes widened as she realised the boat's significance. "I can't believe you remembered."

"It's not quite a catamaran," Gabe said.

"No, it isn't," Hannah replied, her heart melting. "It's better."

Hannah sighed contentedly, as she and Gabe lay on the blanket staring up at the stars. Listening to the lapping water, she appreciated the amount of thought Gabe had put into their first date. The rowing boat, the hand-in-hand stroll around the lake, the most sophisticated and grown-up picnic Hannah had ever experienced...

Forget ham sandwiches and plastic plates. Gabe had gone for baguettes and a charcuterie board featuring cured meats, a variety of cheeses, olives and honey. Instead of crisps, he'd brought popcorn and chocolate-covered strawberries. All of which were served on proper crockery, to eat with real silverware. Gabe had even packed two crystal glasses for the sparkling wine that accompanied his food.

"Did you know shooting stars can come in different colours?" Hannah asked, continuing to look at the night sky. "According to the minerals the rock contains."

"I didn't know that, no," Gabe replied.

"For example, iron, which is one of the most common metals found in meteoroids, glows yellow when it burns. Those with a high calcium content can appear purple."

"Where do you learn all these facts?" Gabe's tone was a mix of admiration and confusion.

Hannah shrugged. "Books, stuff I read on the internet, conversations I have."

Gabe twisted onto his side and hunching onto his elbow, rested his head in his hand.

Feeling his stare, Hannah looked back at him. "What?"

"Thank you."

Hannah shifted round too, mirroring Gabe's position. She didn't understand the source of his appreciation. It wasn't as if she'd contributed to the evening. "For what? This is all down to you."

"For tonight. For being here."

Holding his gaze, Hannah took in his sincerity. She felt the wall she'd built around her heart crumble away. Her pulse quickened as she took in Gabe's obsidian eyes and full lips and in that moment she wanted nothing more than for him to kiss her. A little voice dared her to make the first move, while another screamed for her to do no such thing. Hannah tentatively lifted her hand and placing it against Gabe's cheek, she drew his face closer.

"Sure about this?" Gabe asked, appearing as nervous as Hannah felt.

Hannah nodded and as their lips met, she found herself lost in the gentlest and most perfect of kisses.

THE END

ACKNOWLEDGEMENTS

I'd like to start by thanking everyone at Bloodhound Books. Especially Betsy and Fred for your unwavering support in my writing journey. Morgen, Shirley, Tara and Hannah, you're a great team to work with. Without your guidance, hard work and dedication, I wouldn't be the writer I am. You're all fabulous!

A special mention goes to one of my oldest friends, Maria Holden. Thank you for sharing your experiences of working with a personal trainer. I'm still giggling at the image you created for me – red-faced, struggling to breathe, cap pulled down in the hope of no one recognising you. Well done for sticking with it and achieving your goal. When it comes to running, you're a better woman than me. Although thinking about it, you're probably better at lots of things.

Another big thank you goes to fellow author Christine Stovell. *Running Kind* might not have inspired me to don a pair of trainers, but it did inspire me to write Hannah's story. Who knows, maybe my next character will be a swimmer!

Finally, I couldn't go without saying thank you to every single one of my readers. Without you I wouldn't be doing the job I love. I hope my stories continue to make you laugh and, at times, cry. And that they take you to the same happy place they take me as I write them.

Happy reading, everyone!

Suzie x

A NOTE FROM THE PUBLISHER

Thank you for reading this book. If you enjoyed it please do consider leaving a review on Amazon to help others find it too.

We hate typos. All of our books have been rigorously edited and proofread, but sometimes mistakes do slip through. If you have spotted a typo, please do let us know and we can get it amended within hours.

info@bloodhoundbooks.com